THE NATIONAL TELEPATHY

First published by Charco Press 2024
Charco Press Ltd., Office 59, 44-46 Morningside Road, Edinburgh
EH10 4BF

Copyright © Roque Larraquy, 2020
First published in Spanish as *La telepatía nacional*
(Buenos Aires: Eterna Cadencia)
English translation copyright © Frank Wynne, 2024

The rights of Roque Larraquy to be identified as the author of this work and of Frank Wynne to be identified as the translator of this work have been asserted by them in accordance with the Copyright, Designs and Patents Act 1988.

All rights reserved. This book is copyright material and must not be copied, reproduced, transferred, distributed, leased, licensed or publicly performed or used in any way except as specifically permitted in writing by the publisher, as allowed under the terms and conditions under which it was purchased or as strictly permitted by the applicable copyright law. Any unauthorised distribution or use of this text may be a direct infringement of the author's and publisher's rights, and those responsible may be liable in law accordingly.

A CIP catalogue record for this book is available
from the British Library.

ISBN: 9781913867904
e-book: 9781913867911

www.charcopress.com

Edited by Fionn Petch
Cover designed by Pablo Font
Typeset by Laura Jones-Rivera
Proofread by Fiona Mackintosh

Roque Larraquy

THE NATIONAL TELEPATHY

Translated by
Frank Wynne

The school of psycho-physiologists, including Taine, Ch. Richet, A. Binet, P. Janet, etc., are prepared to attest that certain people are capable of automatic writing but, rather than attributing this to the intervention of some external intelligence, they see it simply as a symptom of mental illness, of a disintegration of the personality. Those individuals capable of automatic writing have suffered a split in their consciousness such that a part of the self has thoughts that conflict with the real self and, instinctively, has set down this thought as writing. This bizarre explanation was first propounded some twenty years ago, and this mysterious 'other' consciousness has been given a variety of names: the Unconscious, the Subconscious, Secondary Personality, Subliminal Consciousness, etc.

Gabriel Delanne
A Research into Mediumism

A dog that feeds and licks its balls, is quick to heed its master's calls and deftly licks the hand that feeds with the tongue that licked his bung.

Popular tongue-twister

CONTENTS

ONE
Peruvian Rubber Company 3
Assistant to Amado Dam 11

TWO
Amado Dam 69

APPENDICES
National Telepathy Commission 125
President of the Nation 127
His Excellency, The Provisional President
of the Nation 135
The Intrusionists 141

ONE

PERUVIAN RUBBER COMPANY

Iquitos, August 5, 1933

Señor Amado Dam, with the references here enclosed, I humbly place myself at your service. I am a specialist in the science of race. Since 1902, I have been rounding up Indians in Peruvian Amazonia on behalf of the Peruvian Rubber Company. The Indians work with us in the extraction of rubber and other tree gums.

I flush them out with the help of a cartographer and a military unit of twelve men who use machetes to slash a path through the tangle of vegetation. The Indians live amidst clouds of flies, sorely bitten. The jungle is the sole stimulus familiar to their experience, nor have they ever seen the White Man. They believe rifles sprout from our arms, that we are dead, that we are pigskin creatures of human appearance, or deformed humans.

To appear before them in an attitude of submission, offering foods, as was the practice of early collectors, is a mistake that resulted in heavy casualties. We fire into the air, instilling fear at first contact, and this has saved our lives.

In the main, they are placid and peaceable, but there are brutish tribes. I have waged war upon the Moene tribe, who silently lie in wait and kill without ever showing themselves. Their penises are attached to a fibrous belt knotted around their waist, and their testicles – occasionally decorated – are ostentatiously on display; they demonstrate great stealth when moving through the tangled vegetation, but in open country, fighting face to face, we were able to bring down fifty Indians with one swift kick to each.

We offer them the choice between migrating to the north or working for the company.

While they are being transported to the extraction area, we teach them Christian words and a repertoire of new gestures. How to point at what they want, not to stick out their tongue, not to touch themselves.

We do not rely on slave labour. We pay the Indians with food and clothing rations since they have little concept of money, and are all but ignorant of the idea of private property, although – like hyenas – they are inclined to thieving.

The Peruvian Rubber Company can offer you precisely the resources you require, with full transparency and in accordance with the laws of the sovereign state of Peru as you have requested. We are confident that you will be satisfied with the present consignment.

We humbly remind you that the Peruvian Rubber Company assumes no legal responsibility for the Indians while they are on Argentine soil.

You can rely on us to meet all your future needs.

With regards to the questionnaire that we have received from you concerning the qualities of the Indians and the verbal contract between the Indians and you:

The present consignment comprises nineteen Indians, twelve males ranging in age from fifteen to thirty years, and seven women of childbearing age. The group was acquired on the borders of Brazil. Based on physical similarities, we assume that among them there are male siblings, and possibly a mother, who receives special attentions from the others, but there is no way of corroborating this assumption since virile seed is shared among the tribe as community property.

With them was a baby of some three or four months whom we decided to separate from the group and leave in the care of Indians already settled on the rubber plantations. We felt it unwise to submit the child to the rigours of the journey. The Indians did not notice the baby's absence, and no one cried for it.

We share no common gestures, not even the palm held aloft in salutation. By way of greeting, the Peira people pretend to sniff their armpits and faint from the smell. Others display their anuses. The Arache people, a pygmy tribe who live with their feet in the mud, cover their faces. We have not remarked any of the aforementioned gestures in the consignment we have dispatched.

None of the intonations of their language sound remotely familiar. I have noticed that they do not indulge in casual speech, and the longest exchanges between them are those that follow the crash of thunder or some chance event that spurs them to speech.

One disagreeable feature to which I feel I should alert you is that they are unable to hold in their urine while asleep. In their natural habitat, this poses no issue since it seeps into the soil, but on waterproof surfaces it can cause a problem. More developed brains trigger the command to wake in order to void the bladder, an essential reflex in the modern world. This group of humans, in accordance with your explicit request, is as primitive as may be found in the area.

We have kept them insulated from White Men, and from the word of God, as you stipulated, but it has proved impossible to make them grasp the finer details of the contract you propose, since in order to do so, they would need to understand the concepts of law and country, and first and foremost the notion of difference, of which they are deprived by virtue of inbreeding; nonetheless they do understand that we do not force them to dress, to work, or to do anything other than be where we tell them to be. As such, the essential core of the contract is understood.

Since we encountered them, they have performed no rituals or ceremonies. They have kept us at a distance from a piece of wood that resembles a shell or the stump of a tree. They drag the object around with them with a carelessness that might seem unfitting for an object of worship, but the gods of these people from Amazonas, like their consciousness, predate form, so we have packed it with especial care and included it in the current shipment, which I will now detail:

The abovementioned sacred object.

A collection of bead necklaces.

A collection of dark wood nose-bones.

A humble collection of weapons comprising two spears and a blowpipe whose surface is carved with crosses and lines and decorated with the same black pigment they use to tattoo their skin, which pigment we have been unable to obtain since they have no belongings, keep nothing about them, eat what is to hand and drink directly from the ground. This further explains the lack of any earthenware items in the shipment.

We have included a bag of bones that they leave strewn around after they have eaten so that you might study them at your leisure.

The itinerary for the journey is as follows: from Iquitos, overland, across the Brazilian border and on to Tonantins; by river down the Amazon to Manaus; transfer to the SS Sertoes, third class, stopping at Fortaleza, Recife, Rio de Janeiro and Montevideo for delivery in Buenos Aires between 22 and 30 September. The projected travel time is forty days.

Regrettably, for urgent personal reasons, I will be absent at the scheduled time of delivery. I sincerely apologise for any inconvenience.

    Yours faithfully,
       D. Ontivero
       Peruvian Rubber Company

P.S.: We are in possession of a group of African Negroes recently arrived in Brazil who may perchance be suited to your new undertaking. If this should be of interest, please do not hesitate to contact us to arrange a new consignment.

ASSISTANT TO AMADO DAM

Buenos Aires, 19, 20 and 21 September 1933

The Indians have arrived. We are heading down to the port with Dam to welcome the Indians.

Dam asks me to ask the driver to go faster. Ever since he fired the previous chauffeur, he avoids any direct conversation so that he does not become attached.

We had a call from the port at 6.00 a.m. The boat arrived ahead of schedule. We had not time to breakfast or even comb our hair. As we were leaving, we passed the postman bearing the greasy envelope from the Peruvian Rubber Company and Dam said that he would rather read the letter en route, though he now says that he cannot read for the swaying of the car and has asked me to read it to him.

My reading is almost perfect, except for an initial hesitation on how to pronounce the English word *rubber*.

The contents of the letter make him uneasy. From an attaché case, I take the menthol fragrance he uses when he is nervous. Without looking at me, he stretches his neck and allows me to dab a little on him. As I squeeze the atomizer, my hand is jostled as the car jolts over the cobblestones. The mentholated cloud in the face makes him cough. He calls me a fool. We have to roll down the windows. The breeze disperses the scent throughout the car, perfuming the chauffeur and me.

It is the first time I have ever been aboard a ship. We follow the captain down into the hold. This is also the first time I have ever seen a captain in the flesh.

The Indians have spent the whole crossing cooped up in this pigsty. It is singularly noisome. I remind the captain that Señor Dam paid for them to travel third class.

The captain says that he could not allow them to travel in third class because they refused to wear clothing. He put them in the cargo hold and had them wait on him. Twice, he cleared the decks so that they could come up to see the sea, but they refused. They ate the same food as the other members of the crew, an egalitarian gesture he now regrets since in the first few days they left the cargo hold spattered with excrement. Nonetheless, he had them hosed down once a week because he is an honourable man and believes that this was what they had requested when they mimed swimming underwater.

Dam asks me to give the captain a list of his shortcomings in providing the service for which he was paid. I improvise: the Indians did not have access to the same services as the other third-class passengers. They were forced to make the crossing in a windowless cargo bay, in the freezing cold and in deplorable sanitary conditions.

The captain repeats the word *deplorable* in a mocking tone, as though my voice had the simpering quality of a woman or an invert.

The blinding glare of the deck begins to fade. I can see the captain more clearly, I see part of the Indians huddled in a corner of the hold, their hairless legs, their genitals. Tribal tattoos and scarifications run from the napes of the necks down their spine and disappear between their buttocks. In the artificial light they look bluish.

How to persuade them, with no common tongue and in the teeth of the evidence, that they are not captives, nor enslaved to anyone. I would like to say 'Welcome'. It occurs to me that perhaps if I raise my arms in a gesture of embrace, they will get the idea.

These Indians have no surname. The immigration officer says that, without a surname, he cannot register their arrival in the country. He shows us the identity documents on which are listed their original name (Moé, Itete, Pirá, a babble of sounds) and next to them, in brackets, their Christian name, which, we are assured by the official seal, is a faithful translation of the former. Itete, for example, is John. But there are no surnames. As a result, the Immigration Service is obliged to quarantine the Indians with other undocumented foreigners.

Dam tells me that the Peruvian ambassador gained a reputation for unseemly behaviour during a presidential gala at the Teatro Colón. Dam has had occasion to speak to him; he is a good man. He tells me to call the embassy, say that I am calling on behalf of Señor Amado Dam, to brandish his name, to wield it like a sword and slash though Peruvian bureaucracy.

Swords, bureaucracy. The expression in his face signals that he has recovered his good spirits.

On the telephone, the Peruvian embassy pledges to identify and resolve the problem within five hours.

We are taken to the dormitory in the Immigrant Hostel where the Indians have been billeted. Dam has had a small armchair he spotted brought from the hotel lobby and is having it placed next to a window.

The Indians do not turn to look at us, nor do they react to the noise of the chair being dragged.

Dam says that their disinterest is actually a rather civilised, trusting gesture, because they know that we are not going to harm them.

How could they possibly know? I see it as a gesture of defiance.

Dam settles himself in the armchair and tells the bellboy to leave us and close the door behind him. He gestures for me to sit on the armrest. He wants to determine whether we can share a space with the Indians without need of guards.

I remind him that I have contracted the services of Sanchez Jaruf & Sons, Security Agency a week earlier.

He taps my chin. Those bloody Turks should have provided us with an escort when we arrived; they would be in this room right now, protecting us, always assuming I had come up with a contingency plan, but obviously I have neither foresight nor an understanding of the word contingency.

This is untrue.

It is he who, overtaxed as he is, takes responsibility and takes care of us both.

There was no way to get in touch with the agency as they had just moved to a new building and had no telephone line installed.

In which case I should not have hired an agency with no telephone. He cannot understand why, given all the services the city has to offer, I chose the most basic. After all, this is not Cairo. He mentions the exact amount of money I earn each month. He says that I have no flair for contracting services, given that I also failed in my choice of the company who transported the Indians in such hugger-mugger fashion.

His eyes are smarting, there was something like pepper dust floating in the cargo hold. He asks me to get up from the armrest, leans back in the chair and does not look at me again.

It takes some three hours for the Peruvian ambassador's solution to arrive in the form of this letter, which we receive having not moved from our several positions nor exchanged another word.

He asks me to read it to him.

> Señor Dam, my dear friend. You will note from my greeting and from the absence of an official letterhead that this letter is an expression of my heartfelt willingness to take all necessary measures to expedite a prompt solution to the problem referred to the Embassy by you. I beg you to excuse me for not meeting with you in person, and for the limited options I can offer you, subject as I am to the sovereign laws of the Republic of Peru.
>
> The Indians can be exempted quarantine provided that they reside within the bounds of the City of Buenos Aires with the consent of a legally responsible adult of Argentine nationality.

All documentation must be regularised within ten working days from today to forestall triggering the deportation clause.

I undertake to find these missing surnames where they have been lost. With the help of Almighty God, I should be able to provide you with the surnames before the deadline stipulated by law.

Cordially yours.

Dam asks me to make a note. The transfer of the Indians to Tandil farm is to be rescheduled for two weeks from now. The obvious solution would be to heat the dining hall at Dam Refrigeration Systems and have the Indians stay there, far from any neighbours, in the Hurlingham industrial zone, but that is beyond the bounds of Buenos Aires. For the good of the project, everything must be done according to the law. According to the law, is that clear? For his part, Señor Dam is considering taking them back with us to his apartment in Recoleta. He feels it would be an excellent opportunity to observe them at close quarters and to keep them safe. To cohabit for a time. He wants to show the Committee that they behave well, that they are sensitive to politeness.

But we have no idea whether they have any such sensitivity.

He says that in the past two hours, they have learned to form a line without having to be ordered, and to cover themselves with their hands, and they have suffered the wait like gentlemen. They are very bright. We would have to move them into the servants' service wing, as Hunt did with the Igorots.

I remind him that Hunt had a Filipina wife who

could communicate with the Igorots. Such things make a big difference.

Hunt was a widower by the time he took the Igorots to New York. I should not talk such rubbish. And while the Igorots were living with Hunt, everything went smoothly.

But Hunt took his Indians to a huge house with extensive grounds. He did not put them up in a tenth-floor apartment on the corner of Callao and Santa Fe.

But Señor Dam has made his mind up. He intends to take the Indians with us. He asks me to ask the maids to vacate the servants' wing. The Committee cannot know that we have them living in his apartment; not before the issue of their surnames is resolved. We need to bring in the finest expert in linguistics to interpret their language and obtain from them the minimum information required to get this project back on track. He sorely doubts that I would have the first idea where to find such an expert so, as always, it is something he will have to take care of himself. The whole project is in disarray because of my lack of foresight.

The hotel lobby is filled with wops and bloody Polacks, we cannot get the van near the front door, and to get outside we have to weave our way through the crowd with the Indians still buck naked. The White mothers cover their children's eyes. The Indians do not look at anyone. They are biddable, they meekly clamber into the van. They are docile because they trust us, Dam whispers into my ear.

I think it is because the van is motionless, so they believe it is simply part of the landscape. When the doors are closed and it becomes a cage, or when it moves off, they will probably think it is alive. To think as they think, as Hunt used to say, involved regressing to the basest level.

Dam is grateful that I want to think like the Indians. So, ideally, I should travel in the back of the van with them, 'regress' with them as far as Recoleta, on equal terms, as a sign of humility. As their host, he had considered doing so himself, but there is no one from the Committee here to bear witness. Were he to do it, it would be as though it had not been done.

The van pulling away causes a general commotion, two of the females exchange words like splutters, there are sighs, nothing serious. Then everyone falls silent, stubbornly spellbound, withdrawn.

I watch a spider weaving the first threads of a web on the roof of the van above my seat. The spider's labours lull me to sleep. Here I am, asleep among them.

I dream that I am a woman and a younger woman is using me as a side table in a dive bar down on the docks, so customers can play cards on me. I wake to find my fist clenched, and when I open it I see that I killed the spider. It was attracted by something – a trace of sugar or grease, something it could not resist.

The Indian sitting next to me gestures at my face and says something. I do not know whether they are words. He bends over me and reaches towards my eyes, his fingers pinched together. When I warily recoil, he laughs. The other Indians laugh too.

In the reflection of the window, I see that I am wearing spectacles. They are lopsided and about to fall off. It looks as if the Indian was attempting to straighten them. Just in time, I grab them and stuff them back in my pocket. They must have put them on me while I was asleep. There is no other explanation. I am less surprised by the notion that Indians have a sense of humour than by their dexterity in taking the glasses from me and the fact that they understood that they were supposed to be perched on my nose, since it is incontestable that, should one go back to square one, the purpose and positioning of spectacles is not immediately apparent from their shape.

With a handkerchief, I wipe the crushed spider from my hand.

We leave the sleeping Indians in the van and set about organising how to get them up to the apartment. In the lobby of the building, we encounter security guards. Dam asks me to list the terms and conditions of the work for which they are being paid.

Their duty is to protect us and the Indians. Try not to touch the Indians. Address them in a respectful tone. Feed them. Be patient with them. Transport them as and when required. Clean them.

The guards suggest taking the Indians up to the tenth floor via the stairs in groups of three.

Dam is more inclined to use the elevator, so as not to startle the neighbours. The maximum capacity is four, three Indians plus a guard. Damn gives me a wink and says that he assumes they will think the lift is a cage, or that when it starts to move, they will think it is alive. A bucket will be needed in case they vomit. It would also serve as a defence should they become violent.

I go on ahead, taking the stairs. The maids have vacated the servants' quarters and piled up their belonging in the kitchen. Venancia completely miscommunicated the orders I gave over the phone. She hung up, convinced that the request for them to move was a prelude to dismissal, so she told the maids to pack their bags and help her to pack hers, since she can barely see.

Before greeting them, I make it clear that no one is losing their job.

One hot-headed maid demands to see Señor Dam. She refuses to be fired by me; she does not answer to me.

I tell them again that no one is being dismissed, that this was simply a misunderstanding on the part of dear Venancia.

Another hothead insists that she does not answer to me either. A third is sobbing.

They have got it the wrong way round. Completely the wrong way round. They will all be given a salary increase of thirty percent per day while our guests are in residence, a maximum of ten days. Señor Dam will personally introduce the guests.

Moving from left to right, Dam greets all the maids by name. Sometimes he does so according to rank, starting with assistants and working his way up, he has an exceptional memory. He tells them that he needs their calm and their people skills for a special task, an invaluable urban experiment in cohabitation between different peoples for anyone working in the service sector, the opportunity to become the most highly qualified maids in all of Buenos Aires, and, should they choose, to abandon him – ungrateful as they are – and work for someone richer than he.

Most of them do not understand that *ungrateful* is a joke, so Dam smiles by way of explanation and forces himself to laugh; such things are difficult for him. He asks me to list their revised working conditions.

Minimal contact with guests. Keep them under lock and key and do not open the door unless the security guards are present. Feed them six times a day, with extra helpings if they want more, a full belly is a happy belly. Be tolerant of urine and excrement: teaching them to use the toilet is contrary to the project. From what we know, they sleep on the floor, so it is all right to line the floors of the rooms with blankets. No more than four guests to a room; males and females in separate quarters. Windows should be kept closed until the guests are able to gauge their distance from the city and the notion of a tenth floor.

Now, the washing and disinfection of the female guests. The guards will see to washing the men.

Dam says that the most important part of the new terms is absolutely secrecy. That this secrecy is not an attempt to cover up anything unlawful. That he does not need to remind them who he is, and the values that he stands for. They are not to discuss what goes on here with anyone other than him, me and the guards. They are not to talk about it in the presence of a supplier, or tell a friend, or a member of their family, or even confess it to a priest, since it is not a sin.

Venancia takes the Indian women to shower in the servants' bathroom. They are indifferent to the electric lights, the Louis XV furniture, the hard-edged objects, the hot water, but they are excited by the soap, and allow themselves to be scrubbed by the old woman with an unwholesome pleasure I can see in the way they bite their lips and let their eyes roll back. Clearly, there are some gestures that are universal.

At Dam's request, the Indian men shower in the main bathroom. They do not seem to mind being touched by the guards, who leave them sparkling clean. So much for touching or not touching them.

I personally show them to their rooms and gesture for them to lie down on the blankets.

There are traces of moss on the heels of the feet and between their toes. This despite the fact that their feet are disinfected and in an impeccable state of hygiene. In the jungle, they choose to wander naked, amid sharp and rotten plants, amid the poisons of the animal and vegetable kingdoms. What really shocks me is that even here, in a dry, enclosed space, they feel nothing inappropriate about continuing to be naked. What kind of people, what insensate people allows themselves to be ripped from their lands without a fight.

In one of Dam's magazines, I read that sleeping mammals can tell if they are being watched and wake in order to defend themselves, because a look is a physical thing that touches objects. The Indians do not wake while I am watching them. An interesting opening for a conversation with Dam.

Dam says he can hear a baby crying.

What?

His tongue stiffens and saliva trickles out. The cry of a baby. The one that was mentioned in the letter. Among the bags of the Indians' belongings, in the library.

It must be a ship's rat.

It is not a rat. It is the baby; they smuggled him with them, then forgot, because they have no memory. What need have they of memory when the jungle is always the same. This is why none of them wept for him.

I insist that it is a rat.

The baby must be freed. He asks me to come right away and help him unpack everything. He can see that I am about to go to sleep, and apologises for coming into my room without knocking, but this is something that must be done. What on earth am I reading? A theatrical magazine?

I leave the magazine to one side where he can find it. What good would it do me to tell him that I read his books when he is absent, that I own three shelves of books and plan to acquire more, but I have already spent the money I found on his political atlas of the world. I ask him if I have time to put on shoes.

He asks me to fetch gloves and a hammer, in case it is not a baby. He says the parquet floor is spotless. We can walk around in our socks. He is wearing his socks.

We go into the library. He points to the box labelled 'cult object'. He says that this is where the wailing came from.

While we are searching for the key to the box, which he claims I lost, we hear nothing unusual. I have no idea whether rats can choose to be silent. Right now, that would seem to be the case.

Dam pats me down because he thinks he has seen the outline of a key in my trouser pocket. He rummages around and extracts it.

Inside the crate is something wrapped in burlap. It is quite heavy; it takes two of us to lift it us. We can feel that the padding is damp with a colony of fungus.

I ask Dam to unwind the burlap while I stand nearby, brandishing the hammer.

The object looks like the base of a tree, complete with roots and the stumps of branches, but it is rounded, like a huge walnut shell that could contain many rats, or a medium-sized dog curled into a ball. On the surface, there are various slashes that look intentional. From the front it has the look of a totem or a goddess. According to the expert, it is a religious icon. A minor deity. It could well be.

Dam finds it difficult to see it as a deity. In any case, he says, the faith of these Indians lacks fine motor skills, since even the Pwiggi, the most primitive tribe in Oceania, who worship gods buried face-down in the sand and are forbidden from turning them over, decorate only the reverse side.

I remind him that he specifically requested a primitive tribe.

He repeats my words in a shrill falsetto.

His mocking imitation of my voice is accompanied by a deeper moaning voice that continues to come from within the shell even when Dam trails off, seeing that I am about to cry.

One of the slashes in the wood looks deeper than the others. A notch. Dam sticks his finger into the groove. The shell creaks and opens into three parts.

The breathing thing within looks like a tumour in the wood covered with bristling hair. From this body contorted from lack of space and forced to adapt to the shape of the shell there emerges a leg, a pair of eyes opens where there were none, then an arm equipped with claws of rotting bone leaves a trail of blood on Dam's leg.

The initial meetings of the Committee took place at the Jockey Club, but ever since Rosso became the majority shareholder, they have been held at his house, which is constantly being redecorated, and the evenings are wasted on comments about paintings and upholstery that would match the floor, because Rosso's first decision was the extremely costly dark green marble in the living room and the architects have designed everything else to match, with the result that everything in the house is defined by the floor, including this iridescent teacup, which is green or black depending on the angle from which you look. Bloody dago. This evening's waste of time is a mother-of-pearl cigarette case that Rosso claims keeps the tobacco moist. They all started smoking and not one of them thought to invite the assistants, who are sitting in this corner with Señora de Cabelludo, the stenographer.

Gatto, another dago whom Rosso invited so that he would not feel out of place, burns his moustache as he attempts to light his cigar, a moustache so wispy it looks like scabies that has already caught fire twice during Committee meeting because of its size and because of the wax he uses for the tips.

Liniers suggests that Gatto get a moustache trainer from Harrods.

Plaza claims to have used a moustache trainer every night for a month. It was useless. A moustache cannot be made to grow into an artificial shape. A diminutive hairnet cannot hope to triumph over nature, although the wax has a pleasant fragrance. Eventually, he gave up because the moustache trainer hangs over the ears and the tension of the moustache becomes very uncomfortable.

Gatto asks the Señora de Cabelludo to record this exchange in the minutes in case he should forget the name of the product.

Dam could put an end to this twaddle simply by declaring the meeting open, but he is showing the wound on his thigh to Dr Thibaud, who rolls his trouser leg up over his knee and criticises the bandage I have worked so hard to make.

Dam informs the Committee that he received an initial shipment of artefacts in advance of the arrivals of the Indians a fortnight from now. The most important piece is a cult object in the form of a wooden totem or goddess which, at midnight last night, began to groan and was found to contain a sloth (*Bradypus tridactylus*) in a state of hibernation, within a perfectly adapted chamber, its rectum linked to the outside by one tube, while another tube connected to the mouth allowing it to be fed. The artefact is made up of three component parts secured by an internal net of fibre which can be tensed by pressing a finger into a deep groove. This net also serves as a mesh to restrain the enclosed animal. He tells how the animal attacked him and shows off the wound in his leg. As though we had not all seen Dr Thibaud examine it already. Does the Committee realise that such an artefact is unique in all of Amazonia? These Indians promise to be different from the others, a treat for the ethnologists at the park.

Liniers is concerned that the Committee continues to talk about ethnologists, plural, when one would be more than sufficient.

Plaza says more than one would cost a fortune.

Dam insists that the salary paid to the ethnologists can be as low as the Committee decides.

Rosso rolls in a display case covered with a dark green cloth, sets it in the middle of the group and, with a flick of his wrist, removes the covering, excited by the attention it receives. It contains twenty skulls of indigenous Indians, carefully classified and documented as to origin, which have been donated to the project by Ameghino, on condition that they be exhibited in the park museum.

They examine the skulls.

Liniers claims that it would be cruel to put this vitrine on display somewhere that the resident Indians might see it.

Rosso says the skulls are from Argentine Indians. He does not think the Amazon Indians would be upset by relics of a foreign tribe. In a previous meeting, it was agreed that the resident Indians would not have access to the northern wing in order to protect visitors and the estate.

Dam notifies the Committee of the offer by the Peruvian Rubber Company to supply a contingent of Negroes recently arrived in Brazil from Africa to add to the project.

Plaza says that there are already Negroes and Asians on their way. They will arrive on the same boat as the Mapuches being repatriated from France. He is negotiating with the owners of the former director of the Jardin des Plantes to keep a number of specimens from the Indian Ocean that were left unused after the exhibition closed.

Dubarry asks Señora de Cabelludo to stop recording the minutes. He is morbidly obese and has us almost spellbound because we do not completely recognise him and, at some point, it might not be him. He knows that the Committee is comprised of trustworthy people thoroughly capable of providing the arguments he will not use, to be crude. He is against the inclusion of Negroes because the common people associate them with slavery. Hostile members of the press might describe the project as little more than human trafficking, which would result in serious damage to his reputation as a Senator.

Bosch brings up a hypothetical issue raised in past meetings of a Negro raping or killing one of the visitors. He wants more money spent on security. He is sceptical of the docile nature of Negroes.

Dubarry says that such primitive peoples are much less so.

Bosch asks whether it is crucial for the project to include primitive Negroes.

Liniers calls for Señora de Cabelludo to resume taking the minutes. He insists that after a few months of eating White food, any Indian or Negro will develop morals and manners. That it has ever been thus.

Bosch raises the subject of the language barrier: there can no morality without a common tongue.

Liniers says that language will come sooner or later. Physical proximity is how languages spread. Given enough time, everyone in the same small space will end up speaking the same language. This occurs because vocabulary is the echo of a stimulus that exists beyond consciousness, proof that the outside world exists and acts upon us. Words come from without. The first ape that buries its feet in the sand is given a word that separates the action of burying its feet in the sand from any other action. It uses this verb and transmits it to other apes as a concept that requires no experience to be formulated.

Señora de Cabelludo whispers in my ear that no Western language contains such a verb.

Plaza says that the process is precisely the opposite: words precede the world, they create it. He offers the example of a deaf Jewish man who learned to speak Yiddish through sign language.

Liniers says that he finds the example of a deaf-mute bewildering and in poor taste. Several members of the Committee snort in agreement.

Rosso says he would not be at all surprised if the bond between words and the world did not exist at all.

Gatto says that with no Negroes there is no business. Nobody would travel all the way to Tandil just to see some Indians. When he was a boy, he says, Buenos Aires was full of Negroes. Teeming with them. Now that there are none, they are seen as exotic. The real interest of an Anthropopark is in the African section.

Dam reminds him that a decision was taken at the last meeting to refer to it as an Ethnographic Park, not an Anthropopark. He is concerned that the Committee has still not realised the gravity of having the letters *opopa* in the middle of the word.

Rosso asks the architect whether the project has made contingency plans for a Negro uprising.

The architect brings a maquette into the room and explains the project. It is the third time this month that he has done so. Excepting Dam and a few others, the members of the Committee are not always the same, especially Dubarry, so everything has to constantly be explained from scratch.

Amado Dam's farm in Tandil occupies a plot of nine square kilometres. Thirty percent of this is exposed low granite hills, a further twenty percent is native forest, irrigated by a river with a central lake of about four hectares, the rest is grassland. It is the largest estate in the world dedicated to this kind of development. As he says this, he holds up his hands. The entrance to the estate will be a huge gate of composite marble carved with allegorical figures together with a sculpture that, to Dam, is both a metaphor and a synthesis of the project: *Chronos pacifying the people of Atlantis*. He produces the new estimate for construction costs and asks that it be reviewed and approved today. From the gate, it is a kilometre to the Danish-style mansion which he is refurbishing with embellishments and a mansard roof in the French style. The mansion will serve as a reception area for visitors. Construction is almost complete. In the grounds to the rear of the house is a temporary accommodation which will be used to house the first residents once wiring has been completed. The annexes containing the research centre and the museum are still in the planning stage, waiting for the Committee to provide funding for their construction.

Today, the architect is proud to present Stage Three of the project. On the western edge of the maquette, in an area of dense forest, is the American Pavilion adorned with bas-reliefs that echo the lush jungle, together with an annex for housing national Indians decorated with an outline of the Andes. To the south, the African Pavilion, whose entrance is guarded by misshapen wooden idols. To the east, the Oceania Pavilion, as orange as the deserts of Australia. To the north, between the granite hills, the Asia Pavilion, with Indian-style friezes topped with a spire in the form of a pagoda. Depending on the budget allocated by the Committee, the pavilions will be clad either in stone or in *carton pierre*, like the pavilion in Coney Island. Europe and Antarctica have been excluded since they have no ethnic tribes of interest, but if at some point Eskimos should become available he would consider adding a North Pole Pavilion. The overall design, he explains, relies on fantastical ornamentation in order to enhance the visitor experience and make it clear that these are modern living quarters that shelter the resident Indians from the vicissitudes of their natural outdoor habitat.

Rosso leads a round of applause for the architect's maquette. He suggests that the Indians could help build the rest of the park in order to minimise costs, keep them occupied until the opening, and, through work, foster a sense of belonging to their new home. There is, he says, no more dignified means of fostering a sense of belonging.

Dam argues that the Committee has a responsibility not to repeat the mistakes made by European parks. The Indian should not, as Rosso suggests, be turned into a common bricklayer. The Indian must remain Indian. This is an axiomatic part of the project. Another axiom: given the unavoidable contact between us and the visitors, the conservation of the Indian can only be artificial. The primary duty of the Committee, the only one that will ensure a profitable business within the timeframe, is to let the Indian lead the life he already knows and only resolve those issues he cannot understand, behind the scenes, as swiftly as possible, reducing any contact to the strictly necessary, such as a medical emergency. He cannot imagine any situation that would require a greater level of contact. What the Indians need can be delivered by indirect means. Leave them to forage for food left randomly around the grounds. Release old cows or horses that they can hunt. Provide them with specific areas where they can remain out of sight of visitors. Ensure privacy. The park cannot become a prison. Either for the Indians, or for the project. The complex in Lyons was charged with flouting the laws protecting free Negroes in French colonies and forced to close only two months after its opening. In Barcelona, the Catholic Church claimed that the Indians' nakedness encouraged licentiousness and that the park was full of middle-class freaks with binoculars who went to look at bare flesh. Later, it was discovered that the park owners were prostituting female Indians, running exclusive nightly tours for businessmen. When the park closed, the local authorities forced the Indians to attend school and learn to read and write. Within five minutes they became Christians. It is vital that the Committee understand that the decisions under discussion are extremely delicate.

Rosso bends over the maquette to take a closer look. The Oceania pavilion is superfluous, he says. No one in Argentina is interested in Oceania.

Dubarry insists that there should be a pavilion of White peoples. Where would such White tribes be found? There must be some in Russia.

Rosso says he is still waiting for the architect to explain the contingency plans for a Black uprising.

For this contingency, the architect suggests canalizing the river such that the pavilions, like islands, are separated by water and connected by drawbridges. A second option would be to surround the pavilions with tall trellis planters of imitation stone, with gaps 'between the branches' affording views of the other side. This would be more inexpensive than digging canals, but the charm of canoes plying the waters throughout the grounds would be lost.

Dam imagines the canoes coming and going with supplies of fresh semen leading to miscegenation between Indians, Blacks and Asians, and the collapse of the whole with a single generation. The continued existence of the park can only be ensured if the tribes reproduce, but there can be no crossbreeding. If people want to see half-castes, they do not have to leave Buenos Aires.

Bosch says that incest will need to be prevented to avoid the park being burdened with defective specimens.

Dr Thibaud says that the presence of the genetically subnormal would offer an excellent opportunity to determine whether the original living conditions of each tribe are accurately recreated.

Plaza finds this idea repugnant.

Dam replies with a motto from his father, Segundo Jorge Dam: 'Listen without judging, otherwise there can be no listening. Respond with judgement, otherwise there can be no response.'

Gatto says that genetically subnormal individuals would add a note of colour, as long as the numbers involved were kept within reason.

These is a discussion of how many genetically subnormal individuals would be considered reasonable.

Conversation circles back to the issue of park safety, of Negroes breaking out and raping. Bosch wants more money allocated for security. Rosso agrees. As does Dubarry, who wants there to be no Negroes in the park.

The scent of Dam's fury drifts over to the corner where I am sitting. Señora de Cabelludo reaches into her pocket and dabs her nose with a handkerchief steeped in some white liquid from a flask emblazoned with the national coat of arms.

Dam pauses and takes a drink to soothe his throat the better to roar. They have been nothing but a hindrance from the beginning, he bellows. He calls them morons.

Around the room, several jaws drop. Dam never allows himself to be seen like this in public. The Committee were not expecting such a reaction.

I get to my feet, request permission to speak, and suggest that we might ask Sanchez Jaruf Security Services to evaluate the safety measures of the project.

Dam tells them to ignore what I have just said. That it was nothing but drivel. The Committee knows nothing about Sanchez Jaruf Security Services. They are Turks. I was simply trying to prove myself useful.

Liniers says that his assistant also tends to talk too much. If he has not done so this evening, it is because he is asleep. He gestures to the man.

Everyone turns to look at Liniers' assistant. I cannot see him because of Señora de Cabelludo's hair, but I can hear him snoring. If I were closer, I'd give the poor man a little kick to wake him up.

Dam emerges from the meeting in a foul miasma. I prepare to spray him with his cologne but he stays my hand. He gets into the car, making the air unbreathable. He asks me to ask the driver to step on it.

The Committee is completely swamped by minutiae, he says. Two years of meetings and everything is going backwards. It would have been better to announce that the Indians have arrived, to reveal that they are living in his apartment, or to have them transported to Rosso's preposterous mansion, so that the wimps on the Committee can see the bare flesh that will be in the background of the photograph taken at the inauguration, the frieze of penises that will be behind them in the photograph for which they are already practising solemn faces for posterity, and he among them, making the same face, a face like mine, it is my fault that he has to come up with an imaginary name for the Indians, that he has to dictate spurious information for the plaque outside the pavilion, that he has laid himself open to anything, to the Indians eating each other in front of a group of schoolmistresses, in front of their pupils, and all because he trusted me.

His tongue stiffens. It rains saliva. He calls Senator Dubarry a fat whore. He compares Bosch to a chicken left rotting on a table for weeks. I have never seen him grimace like this, his mouth contorted into a thuggish rictus.

He removes the bandage from his leg. He does not want me to help him. The wound is throbbing, it feels swollen. He accuses me of putting him at risk of septicaemia.

He kicks the front seat.

I remind him that he refused to let me take him to the hospital. I offered twice. Didn't Dr Thibaud treat the wound during the meeting?

This time, he deliberately spits at me. He tells me I disgust him. He feels nauseous. His face flushes red, as though I am strangling him with my bare hands.

It's not me, it's not the Committee. He needs to vomit. He needs me to help him vomit. To roll down the windows.

The wind blows the vomit back into the car and it spatters the chauffeur and me.

We are about ten blocks from home. I wipe my face with my handkerchief. I feel the chauffeur staring at me in the rear-view mirror. He points to me, his finger at half-mast. I don't understand. He turns around and wipes something off my forehead, the remains of the spider that has been on my handkerchief since yesterday.

If he would just lie still, I would be able to place the pillows properly and cover him up. He is running a high fever. Venancia brings a bucket in case he needs to vomit again. With a sign of the cross, she blesses Dam and the bucket.

Dam asks us to leave him alone. To answer the telephone. But the telephone is silent.

It is ringing now. I answer. I accept a call from Lobos. The voice on the other end is Señora Dam. She has already purchased a ticket for Buenos Aires so she can come and take care of her husband. She asks for her bedroom to be prepared. She hangs up.

Dam wonders how his wife, a pinhead who reads nothing but the glossy magazines in which she appears once a year during the Ladies' Ball she holds at their country estate, a woman who knows nothing about the world outside her home, who has no clear idea what money is and would be unable to explain where it comes from to a third party, can suddenly summon the courage to come to Buenos Aires alone, nurturing a fantasy that she is capable of looking after him, to piss in this place. He asks me to call her back immediately and get her to cancel the trip.

I call, but she doesn't answer.

We speak in whispers so as not to waken Dam. Venancia tells me about the Indians' first day in the apartment.

The maids had to grope around in the dark, collecting excrement from the bedrooms. The Indians sat huddled in the corners, disgusted by their own filth. She considered taking them to a specific spot so they could relieve themselves, but Dam told her not to.

She found a bar of soap that had been stolen and half eaten.

She asked the guards to disinfect the sloth before putting it back in its shell. The animal allowed itself to be manhandled without complaint.

They fed the Indians rice and apples in the hope it would make them constipated. Two helpings or more each. Only one Indian, the female with the injured leg, refused to eat.

They seem utterly uninterested in anything, although one of them, the youngest boy, was drawn to the glittering chain of a little necklace and had to be physically restrained to prevent him ripping it from around the neck of a maid who now says she wants to hand in her notice.

In the half-light Dam's eyes look black. He is talking about a dream in which Venancia's arms are so long they touch the floor, and are sweeping up lint from the carpet. A hollow leg. A wicker boat marooned in the Río de la Plata. A wicker leg. The car here in his bedroom, the bedroom marooned on the river, his face in the rear-view mirror, my face in a hand mirror.

I can't quite understand what he saw: whether he was looking for his reflection and saw mine, or whether I appeared in the mirror as a portrait.

He calls me by my first name. He calls me dear friend.

A year ago, he sent me to his grandmother's house with documents for her to sign.

We were alone, the old woman and I. She traced the first signatures in her faint hand. The rest I helped her sign, my hand holding hers. This physical contact reminded her of some earlier caress. Her cordial treatment of me thus far gave way to something more intimate, by turns seductive and shamefaced.

She offered me a cup of tea. I said that I would make her one. I had an idea that would leave Dam emotionally indebted to me.

Over afternoon tea, I sat with her, and we breathed in the gas I had left turned on in the kitchen. I said my goodbyes and left her in the living room. The 'forgotten' documents on the desk would give me an excuse to come back.

I was only gone for a few minutes; I did not put her at risk. I found her lolling back in her armchair. I threw open the windows, held a flask of alcohol under her nose to wake her, I held her in my arms.

For saving her life, Dam gave me the gift of a hat, but never, before today, did he refer to me as 'dear friend'.

Venancia whispers in my ear: one of the female Indians has escaped. She ran off into the streets, into the city. The security guards disappeared, she does not know when or why. She had come in to change Dam's undershirt and found the dressing room turned upside-down. A pair of trousers and a jacket, a walking stick – the one with a pommel shaped like a duck's head – and a set of keys are missing, but no shoes, no shirts, no underwear. She took the lift down. The doorman was busy cleaning the stairs and did not see her leave.

Dam is still asleep. It's seven o'clock in the morning. I lock myself in the bathroom.

To reach the dressing room, the Indian would have had to tiptoe past Dam and me with silken steps. At some earlier point, she realised that some sector of this apartment, of which she had seen only part, was used to store clothes, and that clothes are cared for and kept. Before that, she had to grasp the idea of a sector. Earlier still, the notion that to survive meant being dressed.

She somehow worked out that key and lock are two parts of a single mechanism.

She made sense of the lift. To understand a lift is to understand everything about the modern world. Perhaps not everything, but an inconceivable amount for an Indian. Such exertions on the brain might have left her exhausted and aggressive.

But she did not put on underwear. She did not realise that under our clothes, we wear clothes.

Where would she run, and why?

Obviously, she is afraid. The sheer scale of things, the traffic, will surely drive her crazy. She cannot have gone far. An Indian female disguised as a White man, with no shoes. She did not understand the purpose of shoes.

Venancia gives me a little medal she has just taken from around her neck. Apparently, I will never find the Indian without the intercession of the Blessed Virgin.

Down in the lobby, I find the doorman, who saw nothing, not even the cane with the duck's head pommel lying on the floor in plain sight. I will have to have him fired.

The wind plays merry hell with my umbrella. I run around the block just in case fear stopped the Indian in her tracks. I walk down the avenue towards the harbour. Perhaps she could smell which way the river was. Why would she head for the river? To swim to safety? She could not possibly foresee the width of the Río de la Plata.

On the avenida, there is no sign of any accidents or delays. She has managed to avoid being trampled. And then gauged the speed of the cars so that she could dodge between them. Earlier, she had to work out that artificial locomotion is continuous, or perhaps she already knew this having travelled in the truck, perhaps she had only pretended to be asleep, all the while paying attention to the vehicle's progress, the straight sections, the various turns, perhaps she created an internal memory of the route back to the harbour, a map that vibrates in her organs, like a map of the jungle. But I don't think she is capable of that.

She disguised herself as a White man so she could pass unnoticed among white people. It's possible that she is being shoved and jostled because her bearing and her gait are inconsistent with the suit that she is wearing, moreover she is not wearing shoes.

The harbour is closely guarded. Let her get arrested. Detained for disorderly conduct. I'm counting on that. Then, later, I can pick her up from the police station. While she is being arrested down at the harbour, I can be more useful if I look for her in the city centre, just in case. I need to go to the city centre.

Luckily, the wind is whistling towards El Bajo, so it catches the back of the umbrella and pushes me onward. This is a good omen; meanwhile, sodden coloured garlands hang from the balconies for the Spring Celebration.

At the crossroads by the Hotel Plaza, two cars are blocking traffic, the drivers are brawling, the pavement is strewn with open boxes, while ladies' hats are whipped away by the wind.

A gaudy little cocktail hat lands at my feet.

As I stoop to pick it up, my blood pressure plummets. I lean against a tree.

The wind whips the open umbrella from my hand and leaves it tangled in the branches.

I catch my breath. I have almost recovered my common sense. I could have taken the car, with the chauffeur, we would be two rather than one, and dry. How was I planning to bring the Indian back, dragging her bodily?

My shoes are waterlogged. Taking them off to empty them, I realise that I accidentally put on Dam's new shoes. The ones I polished for the committee meeting.

People are racing towards Calle Florida. Shopkeepers, drivers, whole families. News reaches me via word of mouth: there is a disturbance at Harrods.

It could be the Indian being hauled away by security guards; the public ruination of Señor Dam's project. The Indian being gunned down; ruination. The Indian in Harrods, prowling among the clients, intent on murder using glassware, clothes hangers, candlesticks, and the knives in the department on the third floor. To say nothing of the English managers.

I get to the department store with no memory of having sprinted two blocks. The front doors of Harrods have been locked with the customers inside. A man is insisting that, in the rush, he was separated from his wife. No one knows what is going on. Through the shop window, I see the dwarf in the little green suit who greets customers pointing to the upper floors.

Rain streams down our faces as we look up and see something moving on the fourth-floor ledge. I press Venancia's medal to my lips. Please don't let it be the Indian. Please don't let it be the Indian.

It is the Indian, wearing a dress she has stolen from the shop.

People scream at her not to jump.

If she falls, if the awning outside the shop does not break her fall, if she smashes into the pavement a metre from me, do I take responsibility or do I walk away without a word? Why don't I walk away right now?

She takes a few steps, bent double by the weight of the rain-soaked dress. Disgustedly, she rips it off and hurls it down at us. The naked Indian and the slap of wet cloth on the pavement incense the onlookers.

She jumps to one side to avoid an arm emerging from the window. We see her calloused feet, her vulva like a black trail tracing the arc of her leap. She scurries along the ledge on all fours like a lizard. When she reaches the corner of the avenue, she stops dead, her head held high, and stares down at the traffic.

It would be useful to know what she did during her dash through the shop, what she broke, whether she killed anyone. Her rain-streaked face on the high ledge gives me no information. I think I understand her better when I cannot see her.

At one of the first meetings of the Committee, Dr Thibaud said that mentally disturbed patients are often hunched over, their bodies magnetically drawn to the ground by an invisible power that forces them into animal postures. The phenomenon is the effect of Earth's gravity on pathologically dense psychic matter.

Almost anyone in the Indian's situation would feel reassured by the sight of a familiar face. Why not her? My face is familiar. She knows me and I can persuade her to come back with me.

In order to gain access to the shop, you have to deal with the dwarf. I tell him that I know this woman; that I can help.

He says he has strict orders from management not to open the doors. He thanks me for my offer.

I tell him that the woman works for me.

He does not know which woman I am referring to.

The woman on the ledge.

He tells me that the wives or daughters inside the shop are being guarded by the staff.

I scream at him that the Indian woman works for me. That she is my maid, that she is insane, that she escaped from my house.

He asks whether she is my Indian.

She's my maid, she's insane. I am not accustomed to shouting, my voice is hoarse. I hear people laughing.

The dwarf poses a question to someone beyond my field of vision, turns back with a triumphant gesture, comes over and opens the door for me.

The man separated from his wife blocks my path. If I am going in, he is going in.

I explain that I'm going in to help rescue the Indian. That I will personally persuade her to come down. Saying this in a voice loud enough for all to hear is a joy offered me by this moment, but it slowly occurs to me that there is no turning back, my voice is thin and reedy and the man laughs, pointing in turn from my face to the gaudy little cocktail hat I've been clutching the whole time.

The dwarf gestures to me. I dash inside. Distracted by his fit of laughter, the man finds himself still outside.

I am greeted by a blond man in uniform. He introduces himself as the fourth-floor manager and offers to help save my maid in any way he can. For the time being, the management has decided not to call the police. With a roll of his eyes, he tells me he has orders to allow me to take the Indian away without further ado as long as I am prepared to pay for the damages.

Of course, I say, whatever you want. What damages? What did she do? We run towards the lift.

The lurching movement of the lift makes me retch. The lift attendant is also blond.

The supervisor tells me my maid ran straight up the stairs to the fourth floor. He makes hand gestures to indicate that she did so on all fours. The idiot is too ashamed to say it to my face.

He asks me whether I feel alright, trying to meet my eyes as effeminate men tend to do. The penny drops. He got this job because he is blond, he has learned to temper his boorish Italian gesticulations, to be more restrained, and this has revealed the pansy lurking beneath. Luxury stores tend to hire pansies. Gath & Chaves is full of them. I step away, but not too far. So far, he is my only ally, even if his motives are repugnant.

The lift attendant asks how I plan to rescue the Indian. From his eyebrows, it is obvious that he is a natural blond, but the hair on his head has paler highlights. Another fairy.

I give a list of my options: if asking her to come back in does not work, I shall go out onto the ledge to win her trust. If this too does not work, I will mount an ambush of some kind, opening the windows suddenly and pulling her inside.

The man with the dyed hair wishes me luck.

The floor manager shows me the damage to the fourth floor. A broken display case in the cosmetics department. Three mannequins with torn dresses that the Indian attempted to rip off. It is not much. She did not kill anyone.

I had assumed that the Indian could not distinguish between White men and women because we wear clothes, and because she stole Dam's suit. It took only a brief moment in this part of town for her to realise that the creatures who are buttoned to the throat, primped and painted, with no legs, are women. She abandoned her initial, misguided disguise and searched Harrods for a female disguise. Impossible to fathom how she made sense of Harrods.

I find the Indian sitting on the ledge, her legs dangling in the void. On this side, everyone is motionless.

The floor manager says he once heard that the only way to save someone who is suicidal is to repeatedly call them by their first name. As an opening gambit, why don't I lean out the window and call to her?

This is what I told him I was going to do: ask her to come in.

The floor manager offers to hold me around the waist so I can lean out and call her from inside, but if I decide to go out onto the ledge, Harrods cannot be held responsible for what happens. There is still time to call the police or the fire brigade.

He pulls up a stool so I can climb up and peek over. He insists that I call her by her first name.

I cannot recall the spit-flecked syllable of her name. What name to give this face, those tattoos, that would be suited to a maid? I draw a blank; the only thing that comes to mind is Leonor, a White name. I cannot call her Leonor.

I open the window and heave half my body outside. The floor manager holds the window tightly against me so as not to let in too much rain. I press Venancia's medal to my lips again. Please, heed my prayers. Blessed Virgin, heed my entreaty.

I call to her: Venancia! I tell her not to move, not to fall. I bring my hands up to my forehead in a gesture of contrition that she understands.

She does not react to the fake name. She would do the same with her real name.

I pull myself inside and close the window to see how I'm doing. One customer tells the floor manager that I should go out onto the ledge and forcibly drag her in. Another tells me to hurry up, her niece is waiting for her outside. This complaint is taken up by various others around the department.

I ask the floor manager if he can attach me to something. He cradles his chin so that we can see that he is thinking. He clicks his fingers: a corset. There is a collection of corsets right here on the fourth floor. If I put one on, he can hook me up to a rope or a belt and attach me to a radiator.

The customers think this is an excellent idea.

The floor manager looks at me again. The sickening craving of the pansy. This time I find his lack of promptness exasperating and I stop pretending that I do not understand his intentions. I ask what he wants.

He is waiting for my approval to put on the corset.

A woman's life is in danger, why would I not be prepared to wear it? Bring it here right now.

He slowly adjusts the laces to allow me to get used to the lack of air. It is clear that he has done this many times on ladies who still wear corsets; señoras with less lung capacity than me fitted into this.

When he is finished, I stand bolt upright for the first time. Looking crushed, defeated.

While he is lashing me to a radiator, I take the opportunity to make the assembled company laugh. I stand in front of the mirror, strike a feminine pose and don the ostentatious hat to complete the picture. Everyone laughs.

I hand my gaudy little cocktail hat to the floor manager and go out onto the ledge.

It is quite wide. I grip the projecting rail, keeping my back to the void. I am only ten paces from the Indian, but Dam's shoes are new and offer little grip. Barefoot, I can make better progress.

I crawl on all fours, as she did, to avoid falling.

I sit down and take off the shoes, making sure she sees my gesture of solidarity. I came out into the downpour to fetch her, I am not a threat, I am sitting in the rain, barefoot like her, what more can I do? Thus far, she turned only to examine the rope attached to my waist, then she lost interest.

From inside, the floor manager shouts for me to call her by her name.

Venancia! I cry, in a voice that should be heartfelt, should stir whatever is human within her, but I feel only fear and loathing and a desire for her to throw herself off. She can hear this, as dogs can, she can sense my underlying emotion, so she does not respond.

Now that she is here in front of me, I can see that she is quite calm. It must be the rain.

From inside, the floor manager shouts for me to sing to her.

Perhaps because I am on the verge of tears, this suggestion seems inspired. But I cannot sing. There is a hymn I can more or less remember in its entirety, but only the words, I have no memory for melody.

I recite the words, affecting a tuneful intonation.

O Lord, that which in life hath made me humble,
this suffering my soul doth apprehend;
O Lord, I am but mortal flesh, I stumble
and without pain, I cannot comprehend.
For suffering is the language of the saints,
the lesson of the Passion of Thy Son
who suffered on the cross without complaint
so, in my suffering, what is lost is won.

I am side-tracked by the gesticulations of the green dwarf down below signalling my position to Dam's guards, who have just arrived.

In my distracted state, I miss the Indian's first words; she is speaking to me.

I cannot be sure that they are words. They sound like vowels followed by a sigh, which might be another vowel but sounds to me as though they have meaning, then comes a plosive sound like a T, which could represent the gap between words, since there are no silent pauses, no shifts in volume, nothing to distinguish one sequence of sounds from the next except this plosive.

They probably speak a language that predates grammar, a collection of verbs and nouns, with between four and ten adjectives, prepositions to indicate *above*, *below* and *beside*, plus two sizes, big and small, grouped any which way, and if this is true, then assessing what I hear in her voice, they can speak only of the moment in which they find themselves, they cannot form clauses or sentences. They grasp at subjects between gaps and the sound is almost lilting, like mine earlier, as though she is imitating me.

I was startled to hear a Spanish word in what she is saying. I don't know which word, it's gone now, but it traced a straight line of Spanish tongue. She carries on in her own language, the sighs and plosives coming at shorter intervals.

She says: *name.*

She is asking my name. I tell her, I introduce myself, which is what I should have done in the first place.

Between words in her own language, she says: *will*, with the vibrato of the W, the I distinct from the L, the syllables in perfect sequence.

This day.

Evil.

The Lord's Prayer. The Lord's Prayer steeped in the profanity of primitive man, poisonous, directed against me – what else? – a prayer turned into a curse.

To counter it, I splutter my prayer, which is mine by right, but her venom putrefies the words in my mouth.

I feel a tug on the rope. From inside, Dam's guards call to me.

The Indian says nothing, has been silent for so long and I hardly notice. With the face of a lamb – if she understood the concept of a lamb – she gestures to the interior of the shop. I clamber to my feet as best I can. Together, we walk back to the window.

The moment she steps inside, the guards overpower her, wrapping her in a fresh blanket.

The customers applaud the capture and me. It is a moment I would like to prolong, but with a tug on the rope the floor manager pulls me towards him and hugs me, pressing his whole body against me, says thank you, and in doing so, I warm to him and allow him to hug me. He whispers in my ear that he already prepared a bill for the damages.

We haul the Indian away wrapped in the blanket. She does not seem bothered at being dragged across the parquet floor. Quite the contrary. We allow her to pop her head out, she looks placid. It is our gentleness, our consideration for her, and the fact that she now clearly understands the contract: she is not a prisoner, nor an indentured servant.

The floor manager has us leave via the back door. The guards grab the ends of the blanket and carry it to the car like a hammock to avoid injuring the Indian. Floating above the street like this brings a sparkle to her eyes that makes me sick to my stomach.

To get her into the car, the guards' first thought is to toss her in with a lucky swing. I scream at them not to do it. They nearly drop her.

She slips from the blanket onto the ground and climbs into the back seat.

I pick the sturdiest guard to come back in the car with us and tell the others to walk back and wait outside the door to Dam's apartment, prepared for any contingency. From their faces, I can tell that they are unfamiliar with the word.

Sitting next to the Indian poses less of a risk than turning my back to her. It is a basic precaution. I tell the guard to sit in the front next to the driver, but turned to face us so that he can interpose his hulking frame in the event of an attack, because the Indian is wily and devious.

The guard says he will keep an eye on us in the rear-view mirror. That the position I've suggested he adopt could sprain his neck.

I tell him to do it anyway, it's only a few blocks. I remind him that it is only a few blocks.

If I tell him, he won't believe me, so I ask the guard to recount the adventure of the Indian's rescue when we see Dam.

The guard claims that he saw nothing, since he was down in the street.

But he saw me, didn't he? Up there on the ledge? That's what matters.

Dam opens the car door and welcomes me with open arms. It is a disingenuous gesture that I have experienced before, it begins affectionately and ends with a reproachful squeeze. But no, this time he genuinely hugs me. I am aching from the bruises left by the corset.

He looks flawless, there is no sign of the human wreck he was when I left. He looks better than ever.

He helps the Indian out of the blanket and leads her over to Venancia, who is standing in the lobby. He leaves her in the hands of the old blind crone as though losing her again would not matter.

I want to tell him what happened.

He is not interested. He says we have a lot to do. But first, I should take a bath and have a hearty breakfast.

It is going to be a long day. He asks me to read him a letter from the Peruvian ambassador. He has only just received it and he does not have his glasses.

I ask him whether he would not rather we read it upstairs, indoors. It's spitting rain. For the good of his health.

He tells me he is positively glowing with health, but woke up with his ears a little blocked. Consequently, I need to read it to him right here, on the pavement, standing as close as possible.

> Dear Señor Amado Dam,
>
> Herewith, I would like to communicate the results of the investigation requested by your esteemed self.
>
> You will understand that Peruvian mestizos like myself, nurtured in the bosom of the motherland, have been taught to despise Argentines, a shameful sentiment, one that stems from a generalized antipathy to the White Man. I am, undoubtedly, an exception, because Buenos Aires afforded me the wonderful opportunity to make your acquaintance and share unforgettable evenings with you, like the evening when you pointed out to the whole crowd that it was easy to tell when I was about to arrive because I was preceded by a cloud of cologne. In the madness of this city, I learned to be a little like you Argentines, who laugh at such slights.
>
> I cite our friendship the better to offer you my company should you deem it necessary to cope with any negative consequences from the news I have to impart, to wit: there is no official record of the departure of nineteen Indians of

Peruvian nationality with the names provided by you, and the Peruvian Rubber Company, whom we have discreetly consulted, denies any involvement in the shipment of nineteen Indians that you claim to have received in the City of Buenos Aires. Given there is no record of their departure, the aforesaid persons never left Peru, never arrived in Argentina and, accordingly, are in no way the responsibility of this Embassy. Given this setback, you will understand that I can provide no surnames, nor can I assist you with the documents required by Immigration. I have friends who could perhaps resolve this situation, but they are less powerful than yours.

May the Lord God assist you in resolving this predicament. My warmest regards.

Dam laughs. Heaps blessings on the ambassador. This letter, he says, is proof that God exists. That God is on our side. He asks me to order a spring lamb from the rotisería and send it to the embassy together with a brief thank you note that makes no mention of the Indian issue, and to stop looking surprised, since he finds it distracting. He will explain all later.

He asks me to look after Señora Dam, who even now is only a few metres away, crossing the street with two maids carrying her suitcases. I am to stop her from unpacking. That is to be my priority until he sends her back to their house in Lobos this very afternoon. All this he says loudly enough for her to hear.

She rolls her eyes, shakes his hand by way of greeting and together they walk into the apartment building.

The maids ask me to help them take the suitcases upstairs. I have no reason to do so.

Señora Dam asks Venancia to have all the maids assemble in the drawing room. Nervously, they huddle together in front of her.

Señora Dam tells them she is looking for maids to work for her in the house in Lobos between January and March, offering in consideration a special summer bonus, as part of an exchange in which her regular maids will come to work for Señor Dam here in Buenos Aires. She wants to take them to Lobos to make them a little more refined. She worries about her husband's influence on staff behaviour when she is not present. The master has allowed them to become slapdash and untidy. They look positively scruffy. They will have a much more pleasant time working with her than they do with Señor Dam. Their chores will involve something a little more noble than wiping the master's arse. She is hoping to make them laugh, but the word *arse* fills them with dread. Their manifest discomfort at having to hear the word is proof of how unpolished they are. With such poor skills, who can they hope to serve – a shepherd? She will whip them into shape. Hopefully, they are interested.

Señora Dam asks me to take her to see the Indians. Dam appears and, with a wave of his hand, tells me to take his wife wherever she wants.

Señora Dam sits down among the Indians and, touching them occasionally though without disturbing them, studies their tattoos and records them in a notebook, grouping them according to shape and appearance. After an hour, she says that she believes she has identified a pattern: the red dots tattooed around the thigh represent the person's age – not in years, since the dots far exceed a human life span – but in groups of twelve. They measure life in terms of months.

I am half-dead with sleep. I tell her that it is highly unlikely that the Indians would divide time in such a fashion.

The broken vertical lines tattooed on their buttocks, she adds, asking me to note this down, represent something lost, strayed animals, dead children, crops.

I highly doubt that the Indians are in the habit of recording lost things.

Did I sleep well? I look a little the worse for wear. Why don't I write down what she has just said and then go take a bath, as her husband suggested?

I emerge from my shower shattered. I ask Venancia where the Indian is.

The master installed her in the library.

I go into the library. Dam and the Indian are listening to classical music on the gramophone. He is sitting in his armchair, she is perched on the window sill, looking out. They do not notice my arrival.

I find this tableau of old friends listening to Brahms deeply unpleasant. Aside from the image itself, there are a number of things I dislike. The Indian's sweat in the air of the books. The pop and scratches in the music. Dam never remembers to blow on the gramophone records before playing them, so they get scratched. Surely his priority should be to console me? To ask for my version of events? But it seems his priority is to listen to a scratchy recording of Brahms with the Indian witch who almost ruined everything. Music hath charms to soothe the savage breast. Brahms as a means of giving her a glimpse of what civilisation is. What a stupid idea. What a stupid old man.

I sit on a bench and struggle with my feeling of revulsion. Blood pressure again.

They turn their heads. They look at me with the same pitying expression, touched by my sorry state but with no intention of helping.

Dam says he has something important to tell me.

From where I am sitting, I can't hear him. I ask him to turn the music off.

Precisely because there is music playing, he asks me to get up and come over. It is important we have this conversation, and with music.

I can barely hear him. He moves his lips so I can read them. He tells me that his father, Segundo Jorge Dam, used to say that the privilege of being a rich man is having two right arms. A right arm is not created overnight, you must be wary to avoid the wise guys, the money-grubbers, the lickspittles, the sycophants, you must be patient, and be prepared to shine a fraternal light on the member of staff when it really matters. Though he had not expected it, I had become his right arm. My blunders and his tantrums had brought us to this point. What I had done for him today at Harrods was an act of valour he scarcely deserved.

But still I was not allowed to say anything. To tell him how I saved the Indian.

I could tell him some other day. He does not hug me because he can see that I am sweating, but it is his intention that matters. Now to more important matters: the Ethnographic Park project ends today. It has been an unexpected and opportune failure. This has nothing to do with the Indian woman's escape, with my mismanagement of the matter, with the Committee, or even with the letter from the idiot ambassador. Did I send him the spring lamb? I must not forget to send the lamb. From the ashes of this failed project a new and better one arises. One compared to which the Ethnopark is laughable. As his right-hand man, I am to take charge of the first stage of this new project. It will be a painful role, since it will require me to leave Buenos Aires immediately, and not return for a considerable period of time, to cease all communications with family, friends and relatives – although he imagines I don't have many. He knows that I have no living relatives. A loved one? A friend?

No.

Excellent, so much the better. He does not want to coerce me; who is he to ask this thing of me, perhaps I would rather decline?

No.

He cannot find words to express his gratitude. He asks for my complete attention: national security depends entirely on what I do. The crucial part of my task is absolute secrecy. This secrecy is not a cover for anything illegal. He does not need to remind me who he is, and the values that he stands for. From this moment, I am to be in charge of a team of two guards and three maids. I am to take them, and the Indians, and discreetly move to his finca in Tandil. The Indians are to be housed in one of the barns on the finca – whichever is in the best condition. The staff are to live in the house. They are to be prevented from leaving, but allowed to roam the property freely, keeping away from the road. It is vital that no one be seen. This stipulation refers to everyone, not just the Indians. To a passing stranger, the finca must seem uninhabited. I am the only one allowed to come and go, but should do so as seldom as possible. On no account should I admit a member of the Committee; he doubts that any will show up, but if they do, I am to remind them that the finca is his private property and that they are not welcome; the one exception is Dr Thibaud, who will make regular visits to check the Indians' health and to give me money. The most important part of this new project is the shell containing the sloth. I must safeguard the shell. Food and other supplies are to be bought from at least four different shops so as not to draw attention to the volume of purchases. In Tandil, I will be met by Damián O'Dogan, who manages his business affairs there; he is not aware of the project, nor should he be, but he will prove useful to me. He has told O'Dogan that I am going there to take an inventory of the finca. As a matter of fact, perhaps it would be useful for me to take an inventory. The Indians are to be loaded into the van within the hour. The drive will take between eight and ten hours in total. I am to have Venancia prepare three rations of food per person and wrap them for the journey. He will personally talk to the guards and the driver and organise the trip.

Is the driver coming with us? Surely, he has a family?

Dam does not know, it doesn't matter, he will agree to go. The man is a nobody. I am to choose the three maids. Ask who among them is prepared to give up everything for a better salary and leave immediately, regardless of whether they have family, for an indefinite period of time. This is an important detail for me too: for an indefinite period. He is prepared to give me a few minutes to change my mind.

No.

My salary will be doubled for the duration of the assignment. Now get the Indians loaded on the truck within the hour, with their food rations, their belongings, some blankets for the cold. If they want to fuck during the journey, or at any point from now on, we are not to stop them. If they reproduce, we are not to stop them. The guards and I are to abstain from copulating with the Indian females. He forgot to mention that his wife will be travelling with me. I am to drop her off at the house in Lobos. It's a minor detour. If I have not had my oats for some time, I am allowed to fuck his wife, it will do her no harm, and it is the least I deserve, a little earthly pleasure.

His wife, fuck, earthly pleasure. He adopts the expression he has when he is in a good mood.

Two maids agree to go with me for an indefinite stay. The others raise a long list of problems: children, dogs, husbands. They sob to make it clear how much it hurts them not to be able to accept.

One maid hesitates. She says she is prepared to go to Tandil if she has her own room.

There is no time to negotiate with all of them. The other two have agreed to come without a quibble. I have no idea what we will find in the finca in Tandil. I tell her that, as far as practicable, we will try to ensure decent conditions.

Venancia says she has heard that the Tandil house is a palace. There should be room enough for us to spread out.

I have no information on the size of the servants' wing. I make no promises.

Señora Dam tells me that she is prepared to travel back to Lobos with me, but she has certain conditions. The adult Indians can travel in the van. The children are to come with us in the car. A couple of them, at least. She has already sent out to Harrods for children's clothes. She is not going to allow them to travel naked. They are little angels.

I ask whether she has discussed this with her husband.

Of course. We need to separate the children without the adults noticing.

The problem is I cannot work out which are adults and which are not.

She leaves this to me. She asks me to be sensitive. Did I see the guards manhandling the Indians' belongings? They broke two spears because they would not fit in the lift, the brutes. She is not about to let them anywhere near her luggage. Have I packed my suitcase? When we get to the house in Lobos, she will make me a gift of clothes that Dam no longer wears or has never worn. He has some beautiful suits. A little nip and tuck, and I will look like a proper gentleman.

I ask Venancia to take the younger ones aside, but she cannot tell how old any of them are, so she has selected these seven and brought them to the pantry.

Of the seven, Señora Dam chooses two boys who have the typical bell-shaped penis of childhood, a little girl who looks like a little girl from a distance, and the one next to her.

I am left to dress the children alone. By rights, the maids should do this, but they are preparing food for the journey.

There are two pairs of shorts, white cotton vests, dress shirts and tweed jackets for the boys, and for the girls, dresses like those they might wear for their first communion.

I slowly circle, careful not to touch them. They let me look at them. They raise their buttocks, part them for my inspection.

I put the dress over the head of one of the girls and pull it down. She quivers at the feel of the fabric. I cannot get her arms through the sleeves. I leave her in the dress to work it out for herself.

The others crouch down and peer under the dress to see how much of her is left.

I try to get the boys to put their feet in the trouser legs. I mime the action. It is no use.

I close the door, pull down my trousers then pull them up again so that they understand. I command immediate attention. One reaches out a soft hand and tries to stop me doing up my zip. I feel sick.

I grab the boy closest to me by the scruff of the neck and try to pull his shorts on. He breaks free.

I look around.

I try another boy. They find the chase entertaining. They pick up the clothes and run around me in circles, eager to be next to play.

From all the touching, they become aroused. I remain at the hideous centre of these erections, my hands sticky with infantile secretions.

TWO

AMADO DAM

Buenos Aires, 23 September, 1933

Dear Thibaud, I don't like writing, so I dictated this letter to Señora de Cabelludo and asked her to translate her shorthand version for you.

A year ago, I found myself locked out of my house and unable to take part in the national celebrations because one of the maids lost the keys. The following day, you came by, gracious as always, to tell me how they went. I remember your exact words from beginning to end, which were not perhaps your best, your most useful, or your most amusing. You'll say that I am exaggerating, or that I have an uncanny memory.
    You said:
    a street brawl fomented by a pro-government group; rosy cheeked girls fed on milk from Argentine cattle, hips swaying to the drumbeat of marches and hymns, open and available; we flirted and wooed them; the President's speech; local delicacies; the enthusiasm that you and I, dear Dam,
    He was about to continue but choked on a scone, and to avoid spitting it all over me, had the good grace to run over to the fireplace and make himself vomit

into the glowing embers. As it evaporated, the smell of vomit spread through the drawing room.

That last detail makes the whole scene a memorable incident and links it to another, very different incident, that occurred two years ago at a Committee meeting at the Jockey Club.

At the Jockey Club, you were showed me a kinetoscope reel in which a young lady bends over a flower bed to smell a rose then sneezes dramatically. A gift for your daughter.
You said:
It's almost obscene, the woman bending over like that, with that ostentatiously Italian face, but my daughter scarcely noticed that, moreover it's cheap, a national production, and the fantasy is very Argentine, those ample buttocks.
Just then, my assistant who was bringing our drinks lost his balance and flapped about trying to snatch the glasses in mid-air between cat-like mewls that we found most amusing. You managed to stifle a laugh, because yours is the loudest and most contagious laugh in the Committee and would have spread around the room like a derisory taunt at a working lad. My assistant managed to catch the glasses without spilling a drop and trotted over to us. You congratulated him and accepted the drink with a nod. Then you invited me to come visit some prostitutes in the Armenonville, but I don't remember your exact words, because I had just noticed white flecks at the corner of your mouth, as though you had just vomited.

This is the detail that links this memory to the previous one and the one that follows.

A few months ago, I told you that once, on a farm in Lobos, I saw a squatting woman give birth, with the umbilical cord between her teeth, while my father was collecting the rent.

You said you did not understand why I was telling you this, and your expression fragmented: your eyes still showed a cordial interest in my anecdote, while your jaw was set in a rictus of boredom.

Then I told you that on my wedding day in Mar del Plata, a horse ran to the clifftop and jumped into the sea. It was the presence of my lady wife, who is the devil incarnate. The guests watched as the horse foundered in the water, drinking a wine that I had ordered to be served to liven the mood.

You remained stony-faced. I remember thinking that you lacked a sense of humour.

Your face is linked to the vomit in my fireplace, the flecks at the corners of your mouth in the Jockey Club, and in turn creates three more links: the umbilical cord, the horse in the sea, and the memory of thinking you lacked a sense of humour. These are not useful memories, I cannot recount them to anyone, nor use them for any practical purpose, like the memory of changing a tyre, but they are immovable and, over time, have become the accumulation, the detritus that defines me.

All this is a way to introduce the subject, to remind you, by means of these anecdotes, of the intimate nature of our friendship, to celebrate the fact that we hold our tongues, that we do not betray each other, and to persuade you to listen to what I am about to tell you. I address myself to you because I admire you as a man of science and because you are as fascinated about novelties as I.

We have often spoken about the latest Soviet studies on telepathy. We were fond of them because the experiments included predicting the future with cards, a relic of the circus. We talked about the Russians' deep-rooted love of circuses.

On the morning of 21 September and the evening of the 22nd, the remains of you in me, along with many treasured memories, almost everything, and a piece of my present, were stolen from me, sucked from me by two people. In return, I received their accumulated junk. I exchanged information about the past, physical sensations such as pain and thirst, emotions, the memories of third parties gleaned from previous such events, and various things I still do not know how to define. From that tourism, I obtained almost a whole other world.

A telepathic event. It is this extraordinary incident that I wish to relate to you.

I lied, both to you and to the Committee. As the result of a mistake made by my assistant, the first consignment of Indians arrived in the country a week ago, earlier than expected. Because of his mistake, they found themselves in a legal limbo, and I was forced to take them to my apartment in Barrio Norte. Had the Committee accepted our original suggestion to travel so that we could study the Indians before including them in the park, they would not have arrived anonymously in this fashion.

I knew nothing about them, I could not have known anything about them, any descriptions in the park – the name of their tribe, where they came from, their gods, their relationship to the stars – would have been entirely specious. Some member of the Committee would have devised the hoax. Now, fortunately, the problem no longer exists.

With the Indians came a vegetal object about the size of a dog, resembling a nut or a shell. Inside was a sloth which, when released, scratched my leg. That part you already know.

The animal's curved claws protect porous pads that absorb blood as it drains from the back of the claw. My blood was mingled with that of the sloth.

In the hours that followed, the wound worsened. In my feverish delirium, I saw things entirely new to my eyes, and the smell of my armpits, which links my nostrils to familiar things, abated and gave way to smells from elsewhere.

Beyond these impressions, I was conscious the whole time, and allowed my staff to bother me, asking for stupid, urgent explanations I could not provide given my state.

The fever broke the following day, the first day of spring.

Now lucid, I asked for coffee to be brought to me. The maid, who is almost completely blind, tripped on a little makeshift shrine she had set up at the foot of the bed to pray for my health and spilled coffee down my neck.

As the coffee spilled, so too did a memory that was alien to me, a memory of someone else. It was not the coffee that triggered the memory, I mention it only so you will understand how long the incident lasted.

The memory is stored in my brain like a piece of personal experience. It belongs to an Indian, one of my guests. I am caught up in an action being performed by the Indian, over which I have no control.

The experience is quite as astonishing as you can imagine.

I will not dwell on this.

It is this: he waits all afternoon for the fish to come to the surface. He was told that the river was muddy, but he came here to be alone. A snake slithers from a shrub and bites his hand.

The fear of the snake is my own, it is not part of the memory, but it swathes it like a film.

There is confusion. I know what is real and what is not. The coffee runs down my neck. The pain of the bite is still there, but not in my hand.

It occurs to me that the Indians have cursed me – me, who does not believe in any form of witchcraft. It is a mysterious way of presenting themselves to me and thereby validating their status as victims in this project. My generosity to them so far has been futile. They did not appreciate it. This is what I think, like some peasant farmer.

With no hiatus I am struck by another memory. In this one, I become aware that the Indian is female. I should have realised it with the first memory, since she urinated while she sat waiting for the fish to surface, but did so without touching herself, without distinguishing the act of urination from any other, nor did she think about her vagina over the course of the afternoon, which is unsurprising, so there was no record of it, and I did not feel it between my legs.

In this second memory, the vagina plays an important role.

The Indian is lying on the ground, half-asleep in the sun. Something of her dream filters through, figures superimposed on the landscape.

Two girls throw branches to wake her up. They want her to tell them how far it is to the swamp and tell them whether or not they should go. They are tiresome.

In response, the Indian spreads her legs and makes certain movements with her vagina.

Taking this as their answer, the girls head off to the swamp.

The exchange involves a degree of deliberate ambiguity which the Indians consider a form of politeness, since it absolves them of being reliable at all times.

Thibaud, I am here to tell you that a memory is not a static record of a series of phenomena, nor a narrative piece clearly distinct from others, but rather, as the Indians say, a fever in the body that warms the air.

Memory is decipherable because it is watered by other memories and subroutines of varying intensity and interval whose data allow for understanding. A large amount of information is obtained.

The information I acquired from this memory: when they did not want to speak, the Indians use their genitals to indicate time, distance and mood. The musculature of the genital region is like ours, but with daily training and moisturising, it is possible to make some ten or twelve movements that are used to exchange data. For narration, they use contractions of the anus, which to you would be verbs in the infinitive. Subjects, objects and everything else are signalled using the finger.

With no hiatus, I receive a third memory, which lasts both several days and as long as it takes for the burn on my neck from the coffee to subside. See, the coffee reference is useful?

With their hands and feet, they are digging a large well in the damp earth of the reed bed large enough to fit them all. There are about thirty of them, covered with clay.

It begins to rain. Taking the reeds, they go down into the well. The younger ones bring the reeds to their mouths when they are up to their necks in mud, the older ones wait a little longer.

They spend long gruelling sessions learning to breathe through the reed before they are allowed to participate.

Up above, the old men help to fill in the well by topping large heaps of soil. The mud filling the well is created by the rain and the old men. They toss in branches and other detritus so that it dries hard.

When the clouds clear, there is more than a metre of mud over the heads of those buried, while some thirty reeds steal air from the surface.

As an old woman, I am able to stand above, watching the whistling reeds that emerge from the hard ground and to dig, as the old men do, until those who survived being buried alive for three days return.

So ended the first phase of the incident. I will come back to the subject of phases.

I sent the maid away and wiped the coffee from the back of my neck. I jumped out of bed and ran to the servants' quarters to find the Indian and embrace her, but I did not recognise her in any of those present. I saw strange expressions on the faces of the maids. They were trying to hide the fact that the Indian had escaped.

Luckily, the housekeeper anticipated my dizzy spell and pushed forward a little chair that was already behind me to break my fall.

Let us replace the coffee with the chair. You work out the trajectory of my body as it reaches the chair. Before I collapsed, I received information of a different kind to what had preceded it, a series of physical impressions of the fugitive Indian: cold, sore feet, frantic breathing, the stench of petrol and the urge to shit, all taking place somewhere else — not in the jungle, but a few blocks away, in the shadow of the Torre de los Ingleses. So begins the second phase.

First, a number of clarifications.

To these Indians, what we call telepathy, what we imagine as a mental exchange, is in fact a secretion, something exuded from the body, like sweat. The verb they use to describe it includes the notions of sweating, of vomiting to cleanse the gut of excess alcohol, the idea of looking up and searching for the sky among the branches, and the idea of startling someone in the dark. It is a recreational activity. You and I would call it a vice.

When they feel so inclined, they open the shell and allow the sloth to scratch them. There may be a relationship between the depth of the wound and the duration of the event, but since the Indian does not know, I cannot say.

The only important precaution is not to be scratched twice in one day.

The Indian allowed the sloth to scratch her on the night they were all taken away. Later, I will tell you in person how they were taken. Then the sloth scratched me.

The event creates a link between the last person to use the sloth, in this case the Indian, and the next person to use it, in this case me. Each single wound results in two events.

The first event happened to her and the second, which I was unable to prevent, to a Westerner. I will come back to this.

The event takes place in two phases. In the first, not unlike flirtation, memories gauge the encounter. The reception of the other's memories is simultaneous, passive and unilateral. I do not know which of my memories the Indian received during this flirtation, and vice versa.

The second phase is a shared present. For almost two hours, what the other does, what they think, is experienced by both, as one. The two are locked in an action that is being performed.

They have no control over each other's behaviour, but they have unrestricted access to available materials.

The reason that it is a recreational activity is because the second phase is accompanied by a friction of humiliating physical pleasure that would despoil the most virtuous soul with idleness and lust. It is a devilishly salacious act. While it is happening, you cannot do anything else, because you are in two places at once, because of the sheer wealth of information and the degree of pleasure. It is best to remain seated, or buried in mud, as they do.

The parts altered by the experience are the genitals and anus, the liver, the kidneys, the sphincter, which light up like little lights in a circus caravan, and the sloth.

To the Indians, the sloth is a physical part of the process, one they include among the organs of the body that elders describe to children with their legs splayed.

This is what happens: the Indian is running through Retiro, chaotically dressed in one of my suits. The second phase of the event takes place as she is crossing the avenue towards the Plaza Hotel, whose sheer height calls to her. She has already received my memories and is looking for a private place where she can enjoy herself unmolested and look down on things from above.

Her whole body quivers sensually, which causes a car to crash. I am there with her. The fear of being hit by a car is more mine than hers.

I lock myself in the bedroom so that the maids do not see my erection, and for a moment (what nonsense!), I feel shame for the Indian, but my turgid penis between her legs makes her squirm with pleasure.

While we are doing this, I receive the burden of the city and the burden of being in my house, which she finds horrible.

We head down along Calle Florida through the general commotion. People are not accustomed to seeing Indian women in the streets.

In my mental map of the city, the quiet space she is looking for does not exist. It occurs to her that the only way she can enjoy the event is in a dress. My suit is not appropriate for her. She is intensely curious about dresses; she wants to wear one. If she rips a dress off the first woman she sees, we would have a struggle, dizzy as we are with pleasure. Using my memories, she decides it would be better to go to Harrods. We run to Harrods.

She crashes into the great glass doors. She still finds panes of glass confusing. She touched them in my apartment, and on the boat, but she believes that some of them must be softer, because her first mental comparison was that of a bubble that bursts when it is touched.

The diminutive doorman threatens to slam the door in her face, but she hurtles past him, screaming at the top of her lungs.

No one moves.

She glances around the shop. She can see no dresses. I cannot remember which floor has ladies' fashions. Together we explore the shop from the ground floor up.

With a tug, she rips off my suit. She walks silently, examining the necks and the knees of other customers for the tell-tale muscular contraction that heralds an attack, but they are all slack-jawed, focused on the fact that she is naked.

I scamper up the stairs on all fours. People are screaming now. Seeing a human being skittering on all fours is terrifying. But there is no easier way to climb stairs. When one's weight is properly distributed, the body becomes lighter and moves more swiftly.

I don't yet know whether the searing pleasure that has me bent double is bliss or torture. I am worried about the Indian running amok in Harrods, led here by my presence in her, hindered because I require her to pay attention to details she does not see as threatening, like the sales staff warily following us, huddled into a little group, and by the things that she does not want and I do, like a gun.

She pilfers an umbrella and tests it out, smashing a couple of display cases to enhance the pleasure of the event with an act of violence. Sitting on my sofa, I can give her nothing comparable.

The dresses are on the fourth floor. She slips on a huge one in which she can move freely.

She races to the window. She notes that, above a certain height, the exteriors of buildings are not used. She can see no one walking on the ledges or sitting with their legs dangling in the empty space. To her, windows seem like half-formed doors that simultaneously invite you and forbid you to go out.

From this she formulates five hypotheses:

White people are unintelligent.

White people have skin problems.

They have no sense of balance.

This city was built by people with different bodies of very different dimensions and White people swarmed here, like flies, and live in this city because they do not know how to build a city to their own proportions, and so they obstinately survive in this space that expels them.

I say White people so that you will understand. When she thinks of us, she uses a different word, a verb that describes skinning an animal, and physically she sees us in a garish colour that is neither ours nor real.

Climbing out onto the ledge gives her a moment of respite. She deciphers the mechanism for opening the window without my help, as she did the door locks and the lift when she left the apartment. Compared to the jungle, the city seems simple to her because everything is human.

Sitting on the ledge I almost fell off the sofa. A little joke for you.

The moment she steps out the window, the dress feels like a burden to her. She pulls it over her head and she kicks it down into the street. Some people jump to try and catch it, but it gets caught in the shop awning.

She sits and gazes at the city. She wonders how the world came to be folded such that it could give birth to such a thing.

You see, for them the idea of folding is very important. It is their only anchor.

The indigenous word that corresponds to *folding* comes to me with the sound of the whisperers in the depths of the wells intoning the legend of the primeval folding.

That whisper transmits this information.

On the night when the canticle of original folding is sung, everyone is exhausted, having spent the whole day digging a well to accommodate the whisperers. The singing from the wells is so faint that it is drowned out by the constant rustle of the jungle.

If the whispering cannot be heard, if the music is in danger of trailing off, it is their responsibility to complete the melody. They have known the music and the words since childhood.

The canticle begins, as almost all creation myths do, with references to elemental materials. Water folds upon water to create rivers, the earth folds into basins so it does not overflow, rivers fold over the land and there is mud.

It continues in this fashion for a long time: flatlands fold and give birth to mountains, clouds fold, create other folding things, etcetera.

Once the great part of objects and animals have been born, the sloth folds upon itself and spawns humans.

The first people to emerge from the sloth use stone to inscribe genitals on the blank crotch. The canticle describes nine distinct types of genitals, penis, vagina and seven others, each with possible variations depending on extension, orientation, mobility, irrigation, depth or protrusion. This number is not symbolic, it is the result of direct corroboration of the history of the genitalia of the tribe. This explication is cut short by the lone collective cry in the canticle. Hands sink into the wells.

The canticle continues with the tale of the flies and the city. This section is in the form of theme and refrain that remains stable in its early movements, with the refrain dividing the basic ideas of each section of the song, into something like paragraphs or chapters. As the story progresses, the theme fades and the music is simply a series of refrains, each a verbal mantra encapsulating general concepts for the slower members of the group, and each an associated physical shudder. The words and the order of words in each mantra create a series of impressions as vivid and intense as a memory or a physical experience of the present, although they belong to no one in particular.

The tale of the flies and the city begins with a series of salutary warnings against attracting flies, and a recipe for a healing poultice for the skin.
    This is followed by a refrain that recounts how the first folding of the flies occurred in another place, the result of a different folding, and it was a leak that allowed the flies into this place.

They sing of the whirlwind of flies that all but exterminated human beings. Those who survive, those with thicker skin, lie in the riverbed so the waters can cover and soothe them as they rise.

This passage that I have translated literally for you is the only section in eight or nine hours of singing I can render with no loss of meaning, because of the distribution of sounds and silences that fitted the possibilities of the Spanish language:

They lay covered, as though dead, the waters rose over them, and when they ebbed left them stagnant. Flies settled on them, bit them, sucked their blood, then flew far off to other swamplands, other sleepers. These they also bit.

The people who have been living in the open air find themselves forced to build houses to protect themselves from the flies.

The houses fold and create the city.

They choose a vast terrain of clay, raze it with fire and on the bare ground trace a complete map of the city's canals with undulating lines which, superposed, leave plots of land shaped like a human eye. The similarity is not intentional, merely the result of superposition.

The size of each land parcel is sufficient to build a dwelling for twelve to fifteen people, constructed from wood and adobe over no more than two levels, set on a platform supported by four or more stilts that raise the house above the river's floodplain, each dwelling is surrounded by enough land for domestic animals to graze and an area of virgin forest cultivated to create a garden.

The regularity of the layout prevents the nascent city from developments that go beyond this practical measure which regulates how much can and cannot be amassed and possessed, and the desirable level of population density; it allows water to flow evenly and unhindered during floods; it affords the visual pleasure of an orderly grid in the midst of the jungle. In this last respect, the Indians' sensibility is like ours.

Following this pattern, the channels are dug out of the clay. At the bottom of the channels is a sewage system of earthenware pipes that service every plot of land and divert waste to the cultivated fields. The song explains exactly how the pipes are fitted together to prevent leakage.

The walls of the canals are lined, then the sewer pipes are covered with a thick layer of waterproof white clay which is fired such that it becomes hard as rock. This colour of clay is chosen so that the clarity of the water is visible to the naked eye.

The refrain conjures the image of the canals filled with branches and the night-time blaze that hardens the clay and fumigates the city, ridding it of flies.

Before they flood the canals with water from the rushing river, people climb the trees to gaze down on the unborn city.

The eye-shaped plots become islands.

Dry pedestrian traffic between the islands is via flexible bridges of natural rubber located in what would be the tear ducts. These are capable of bearing the weight of thirty people and can be raised in order to allow boats of different sizes to pass through.

Wet pedestrian traffic is possible via partially submerged sectors that cool and refresh the walker on hot days.

Each island is equipped with at least two wells directly connected to the water table from which drinking water is drawn. The water circulating in the white canals never comes into contact with the drinking water.

The refrain encourages the people to jump and bounce on the rubber bridges, and to use the well water to rouse the elderly with impromptu splashes. This is followed by an incitement to childish behaviour that in no way contradicts the rigorous method applied in the design of the city. Providing free time for leisure and idleness is one of the priorities of the plan.

The song goes on to explain leisure and idleness as a measure of time spent doing nothing or working for pleasure and offers as an example the community care of children once they have learned to walk. Forcing a child to live with the person who gave birth to them is unjustifiable, therefore, once they can fend for themselves, it is best to let them wander from house to house, from island to island, to be lovingly cared for by any adult. The adults' undertaking, which forms the next refrain, is to care for all children with equal attention, not as a chore, but because in the collective responsibility for tasks, the element of individual work is always brief.

The whisperers raise five fingers from within the well. For numbers, the Indians use their fingers as we do. The city is functional for five generations, but it raises these problems:

The waterproof lining of the canals discourages the growth of aquatic plants and since such clean water leaves fish nothing to feed on, they must be caught in the river, which is becoming increasingly distant.

People crowd together, adding additional floors to their dwellings, out of a stubborn attachment to a section of the canal they consider they own, as though the water were not circulating.

In the chafing of the overcrowded bodies of the fifth generation, the flies return, bringing fresh diseases and only twenty people survive, from whom all those alive today are descended.

The canticle ends as day breaks with the melody of the whisperers who are nodding and half-asleep. They tell of the end of the city, which folds into the earth leaving the surviving people with a bad taste in their mouths that has persisted to this day and which, through the song, reaches my own mouth.

The flies triumphed. This is the last refrain, the flies triumphed. As this is repeated, together with the associated physical shudder which leads to frenzy, there opens up a wellspring of information that warns – though the tone is not censorious, but rather humorous – that the tale of the original folding was very different.

That not all were good to one other.

That the period and the location of the city can be easily identified.

That after abandoning the city, communal living and agriculture were forsaken, and with each step, the people commandeered more and more time for leisure and idleness.

That time was devoted to telepathy, which made them increasingly intelligent.

That there was a time when events restricted to two people and the sloth were considered a hindrance by a group of leaders who attempted to create a form of collective telepathy by having the sloth attack them as a group during long sessions that left them at death's door.

That they failed in their attempt, but in doing so, unwittingly reopened the same breach through which the flies first came.

That this prompted the recommendation not to indulge in telepathy more than once in a single day.

The whisperers must now be helped from the well, lulled to sleep, watched over for as long as their sleep lasts, or, if they are not tired, one should talk with them about whatever they choose, agree to whatever they request with goodwill.

That was the information imparted to me by the sound of the word *folding*.

Out on the ledge, the Indian compares the images of that city with the information she has received from me and comes to a provisional answer as to the how and why of Buenos Aires.

I'm still writhing in pleasure like a snake, covered in sperm from head to foot. I resist the suggestion of the sexually lustful Indian who, while she is thinking these things, wants me to suck my own penis to give pleasure to us both.

In the midst of all these wonders, the highest point is a brutal return of the familiar: I see my assistant appear through the window crammed into a lady's corset that is tethered to a radiator.

He, usually such a weakling, steps out onto the ledge, committed body and soul to resolving this disaster he may have caused. The last thing I want right now is to have to take responsibility for his life.

Luckily, he manages to sit down next to us. He does not try to restrain the Indian, or anything of the kind. In a low voice, he sings a Christian hymn.

From this, the Indian draws certain conclusions about White fears, among them that my assistant's whispered singing is a White person's way of shouting. When she compares this with the information gained from me, she comes to understand that my assistant's singing originates in religious faith, and through this the concepts of faith and religion, which are unfamiliar to her.

She weighs them up, delighted by this novelty.

For the common good, she takes it upon herself to calm my assistant. For these particular Indians, good is always of a practical nature. She must console my assistant. Custom dictates she do this by imitating the person suffering. To the Indians, sorrow is something overcome by mockery.

The closest thing to the assistant's hymn that she can find in me is a Lord's Prayer I have never used, and attempts to say it aloud for his benefit.

Snapped out of his fear by the horror at this Indian reciting the Lord's Prayer in Spanish, my assistant slithers along the ledge, squirming and whimpering. At the top of his lungs, he begs to be rescued. It is an extraordinary spectacle.

The Indian realises that her return to my apartment will be complicated. The crowds of people, the man shouting, the cars, the police. She is particularly shaken by the idea of the police, now that she understands it more or less. She should not have tossed away the dress. She regrets her actions, like a Western woman.

Using information from me, she adopts the attitude of a helpless señorita so those inside can see. This helplessness pumps testosterone into the balls of my guards, who are already at the scene.

Firstly, they rescue my assistant. Then they wrap the Indian in a new blanket and drag us across the parquet floor to a service lift, with all the pleasure such a slide can provide to someone who is highly aroused.

Lest you be alarmed, let me tell you that the entire episode was discreetly resolved without the intervention of police or the ambulance service. Your name, my name and those of the members of the Committee remain unsullied.

The event ended during the drive back to my apartment. The last piece of information I received from the Indian was her careful inspection of a pair of spectacles as she sat in the back seat of the car. Caught in the frame of the glasses was a tuft of hair tinted with a blond dye that came off on her fingers. This made her extremely sad, but I had no time to discover why; we were already disconnected.

The organs gradually cooled their ardour. A reviving shower and a shot of liquor. Fresh as a daisy.

I went downstairs to await the arrival of the Indian, longing to embrace her for the gift I had received. One striking fact about the incident is that being immersed in her was not enough to make me love her. One might assume that placing oneself in someone else's shoes is the basis of love and solidarity. This proved not to be the case. It is equally true that the event did not take too much out of me. I felt reinvigorated by the experience of having been an Indian female for a time, but I still recognised myself. That said, what I recognised as mine rather than hers seemed arbitrary and expendable. Fortunately, as the hours went by, this impression faded.

I think that, out of their innate delicacy, these Indians prefer not to be committed to each of the hundreds or even thousands of those with whom they are conjoined and linked in life, such that the event triggers the release of some corporeal humour that neutralises feelings of empathy. Another off-the-cuff hypothesis: this same corporeal humour safeguards who knows which precise elements that make it possible, if not to recognise oneself, at least to recognise the event as being transmitted by someone else.

The Indian stepped out of the car, utterly uninterested in anyone. There was no embrace. I asked that she be taken to a room away from the others, under lock and key.

As in a comedy routine, that same moment saw the arrival of:

My assistant, who scrambled out of the car, desperate to tell me all the things I already knew.

My wife, who is the devil incarnate, concerned by news of my fever, together with twenty suitcases, intent on staying in Buenos Aires until I am recovered, something that will never happen if she stays around for long.

The postman, with an unsigned letter from the Peruvian ambassador in which the bitter, literate mestizo disavows all responsibility for the Indians and indeed the very existence of the Indians.

In simple terms, Immigration registered the arrival of nineteen Indians to the city of Buenos Aires; the Peruvian Embassy denies that they arrived. For as long as they remain in this legal limbo, we can make use of them.

That is why, after a while, I decided to:

Withdraw my personal and financial support for the Ethnographic Park, thereby separating the Tandil land, which is my personal property, from any project undertaken by the Committee henceforth.

Resign the leadership of the Committee.

Take the Indians out of Buenos Aires and hide them on the Tandil farm, together with the shell and the sloth.

Place my assistant in charge of moving the Indians, in recognition of his actions at Harrods.

Send my wife back to the Lobos estate.

Communicate the foregoing news to you, and request that you initiate a research and development protocol for the telepathic event experiments to be conducted between the Indians and the two of us as the guinea pigs.

Extract, together with you, as much information as possible about these Indians with a view to discovering other useful artefacts or abilities.

Identify and record the general principles governing these events with the intention, in this initial stage, of acquiring the fundamental skills to facilitate private and/or state espionage, always in the interests of the motherland.

We organised the departure for Tandil and I took a photograph of the car transporting my lady wife, the maids and my assistant, and the van carrying the Indians, as they drove down the Avenida Santa Fe towards the beautiful woodland park.

All this took place some hours ago. In the middle of the night, I felt my perineum contract, putting my genitals on high alert. The event was about to recur, I did not know with whom. If the sloth had attacked someone, something must have gone awry during the transfer.

I took a pile of towels and locked myself in the bedroom.

I find myself inside an alien memory, the ghostly silhouette of my adult frame in the body of a ten-year-old boy.

The lobby of the Teatro Colón. The boy is climbing the stairs with his mother, a middle-class Italian schoolteacher. It is a childlike, Western memory. The information reaches me more quickly and in greater quantity than it did with the Indian. This is a world familiar to me, the experiment is not wasted on first impressions.

I cannot tell whether the person remembering is a child or a man. Oh, the horror, Thibaud! The horror that a child has been wounded by the sloth and might die from the infection. The horror of experiencing the ghastly lubricious act with a child.

My sole focus at this moment is to avoid embarrassment. The only problem is the mother. She is a music buff. She loudly snorts when she considers a musician's performance wanting. She is hypersensitive and voluble. She would blow a whistle if she had one. I receive a cluster of memories of the young boy's public embarrassment, scenes in which his kindly but inconsiderate mother vociferates at school, in a hospital, at a christening, against the church choir.

The boy does not want her to make a scene in front of the predominantly upper-class audience. The embarrassment typical of the middle classes. It is monstrous that he has internalised it at such a young age. My father, Segundo Jorge Dam, used to say that middle-classness is passed on in the blood as spinelessness.

Before he went in, he steeled himself to ask his mother to be discreet. She promised that she would, but she no longer looked at him, focusing her attention on his hair, patting it with both hands as though it might fall out or, at times, as though she wanted to rip it out. Being made aware of her son's embarrassment is hurtful, and when hurt she is more prone to shouting. The boy feels like a fool for not having anticipated the consequences of his request. His lack of foresight will fuel her guilty outbursts. He could have said nothing, could have trusted her. He has only made things worse.

The staircase seems endless. The boy stops to catch his breath. He notices that mamá's hairdo is the tallest in the theatre.

Down below, a blank space opens up around a naked man covered in tar, a madman. There are no clues in the memory as to how this man came to be in the theatre lobby. People turn away from him with a silent surprise that the boy considers the hallmark of good manners.

If his mother were to turn and see him, she would be the first to scream, from the top of the stairs, the obvious centre of attention; she would shout, not out of fear, but to ask someone to help the poor man, because she is kind, because she has the bovine kindness of a government employee. It is the little boy, not me, who associates kindness with cattle and government employees.

The boy takes his mother's hand, climbing the stairs more quickly so that she does not see, but he does not often take her hand, and the incongruity of his hand in hers makes the mother turn, she sees the madman daubed in tar and screams.

To make matters worse, no one else joins in. The squawk of a mother hen in the Teatro Colón.

One of the staff takes advantage of the fact that everyone is staring at mamá to grab the man's ankle from behind and knock him down. In the fall, the tar-black foot comes away from the leg revealing the necrotic edges of a straight cut and ends up in the usher's hands.

Screams from the usher.

It occurs to the boy that he used to scream like this when he was frightened, but he no longer does so. He is master of himself. Better to learn self-discipline at an early age. His attention is diverted from everything going on – his mother, the severed foot – by the satisfaction of having learned self-discipline.

Another memory. He is walking at night through open country. He is carrying a briefcase. With the beam of the torch, he blinds a cockerel attacking him with its spurs raised.

It is one of my cocks. In his fright, he drops the attaché case, but it contains important papers that cannot be lost, so he catches it before it hits the ground. The fact that the papers are more important than the cock tells me that this memory, and the preceding one are those of an adult. This is not a child. It is my assistant.

He races out and, in the darkness, he collides with me. In this memory I am little more than a formless mass with a motionless face of gossamer skin that is more delicate than my own.

With this memory, the first phase ends.

In the empty minutes before the second phase began, I anticipate the disgust of the ghastly lubricious act with a male employee.

I enter my assistant as he wanders in the cold of the Tandil countryside, with no trousers and a ripped shirt. He has blood-smeared grazes on his legs and his chest. He walks through the abandoned quarry in the moonlight.

Entering my body drives him out of his mind. Inflamed organs function independently of the cold. We could die and the event would carry on by virtue of its own heat.

My wife always tells me my assistant is a pansy. Everybody says so. The joke among the rest of the staff is that he would work for free if I fucked him. But no, the boy is a man. With our double penis in heart-stopping erection, our disgust is mutual, and things are worse when the disgust fades and we are dying of pleasure. This triggers a cloud of subsidiary information that obscures our shared present.

He has never seen a quarry. He is surprised that natural erosion could leave such clean, symmetrical edges in the rock. This is an example of subsidiary information.

I also receive exclusively visual information which, I realise after a while, is a story associated with what is happening, like a narration or a shorthand version of his present, but with words. This is another example of subsidiary information.

I want to know what happened, what went wrong, who fucked up, how often.

He cloaks himself in the idea that he can stay on this side, in bed with me, can flee this nightmare. He crawls under a cubic outcrop of rock, and deliberately recalls his whole day for my benefit.

He does not spare me the episode on the ledge in Harrods, despite the fact that he knows that I was there, with him and with her.

The account of this scene is excruciating. Teeming with adjectives and fear.

He comes back to the apartment. While I am organising the details of the transfer to Tandil and he is hating me for taking more interest in the Indian than in him, the poor thing, my wife – behind my back and brazenly in front of me – devises a completely different agenda, her own, which in the long run brings everything down. She foments mutiny among the maids. She sends out to buy regulation outfits for the younger Indian boys. She makes ridiculous changes to the planned journey. She claims to speak for me and everyone listens. It's not the first time. She has always been persuasive, all the more when undermining me, not so much because of her eloquence, but because she ends her sentences – even her questions – with a positive tone. Such music fascinates the simpleminded.

My assistant follows her about like a dog. To the rest of the team, he is my wife's official spokesman. Contrary to everything that has been agreed, contrary to basic common sense.

He sits the besuited boys in the middle of the back seat with the maids next to the windows on either side. In the front, the chauffeur, my assistant and my lady wife.

The drive to Lobos takes about two hours. His memory contains a very detailed account of that duration. The children kick the back of the chauffeur's head, crawl across the maids, lick the windows, shout and spit at my assistant. At no point do they try to escape, though they could have done so with little effort.

By the time they arrive and are pulling up outside the farmhouse, they have learned to unbutton their trousers and have started masturbating. For the first time, my wife turns around and tells them to calm down.

My assistant does not know the Lobos manor. The house reminds him of the photo of a German castle he saw in a book in my library. In his mind, the image is associated with various scenes – all in black and white, like the photograph of the castle – of him browsing through my library with his testicles in his throat for fear I suddenly come in and find him there.

In the evening light, the sight of the house and the scent of the gardens leave him rooted to the spot, and even when my wife leaps out of the car, sobbing convulsively and desperate for his assistance, he stands motionless, watching her suffering as though it were a picture postcard.

Weeping uncontrollably, my wife suggests he let the Indians loose in the grounds – females in the English garden, males in the French garden – so that they can relieve themselves and stretch their legs before continuing their journey. She will tend to the children.

He does as she asks. He leaves the guards to watch over the men and, heart racing to the point of tachycardia, follows the females to the English garden.

He watches as they piss and shit. The runaway Indian is among them, but he cannot make her out. Their faces all look the same to him.

In the gathering dark, the temperature falls. The Indians are back in the van. The maids and the guards hurried to eat something. My assistant sips a glass of white wine that has just been brought to him.

My wife arrives, her makeup thick as door paint. She always does this to hide the fact that she has been crying.

Having seen the boys in the house, she says, smiling, playing on the stairs, comfortable in their new clothes, she has decided to keep them with her. Ensure they are well fed, healthy, give them work, make good men of them. Besides, none of the adults seemed upset by their absence. They do not care about them. They are not family.

There is a lot of guilty fretting on the part of my assistant that he did not anticipate this last request. To avoid it, he would have had to say no to many of her earlier entreaties. He said yes to everything. Including this.

Before he continues on his journey, my wife invites him to try on some of the suits I have never worn. He flatly refuses. In the recitation that accompanies this scene, his refusal is seen as a matter of dignity. For the middle classes, it is extremely important to feel dignified from time to time.

Between this and the information I subsequently receive, there is a garland of fleeting scenes intended to demonstrate that he has always been an exemplary employee.

He forged my signature so as not to have to interrupt my nap.

He had the blood cleaned off the refrigerator to make my visit more pleasant.

He cleaned my armpits with rubbing alcohol.

I do not think that he is choosing these scenes for my benefit, because in one of them he mimics the way I speak in front of the maids, which is deeply uncomfortable, and in another, he puts my mother's life at risk so that he can save her and win my admiration. Son of a bitch. But I do believe that the information he is broadcasting is governed by his desperate need to ingratiate himself.

He falls asleep in the back of the car smelling the leather seat. He dreams that he is a woman and is hired to be a side table in a dive bar on which customers can play cards. Then he dreams about the Indians playing a practical joke involving his glasses. When he wakes, he is a few kilometres from Tandil.

To collect the keys to the estate, he stops by the house of O'Dogan, who manages my business affairs in Tandil. It is the middle of the night; the city is dead.

O'Dogan, who was sleeping, ushers my assistant into the living room and asks him to wait by the carved marble fireplace. He had it installed last week, he explains. It is the first of a series of improvements he has planned to increase the value of the property.

He reappears some twenty minutes later, immaculate, all Brylcreem and cologne, but no keys. Together they search the rest of the house, and while they rummage through drawers and shelves, O'Dogan spares him no detail of his plans for each room.

My assistant listens, retaining only the bare minimum. That bare minimum is the subsidiary information of the memory. The primary information is his calculations of what is still to be done today. Back in the van, the guards, the maids and the Indians must be freezing. They still need to get to the estate, move into the house, settle the Indians. They have not even had dinner yet. But O'Dogan's prattle means the subsidiary data seeps into his more urgent concerns, and between his conscientious planning, my assistant revels in the tasteless décor of the house and quivers with delight when he sees that the French-style living room does not have two chairs from the same Louis.

Eventually, O'Dogan says that the keys must be in his office, two blocks away, next to the town hall. He insists that they go there together on foot. My assistant agrees.

They trot through the deserted city. As they pass the town hall, O'Dogan stops and pretends to catch his breath so that my assistant can appreciate the building.

Truly, there is no end to provincial pride. My assistant finds the ruse pitiful and, like a backwash, hears his mamá's scream in the Teatro Colón. From this, I intuit that from such simple traumas, the middle classes understand their position in the world.

O'Dogan throws open the door to his workshop overlooking the plaza, clearly no expense has been spared. This was his first major investment, bought before his house. Here, my assistant cannot identify a single flaw.

They come back with the keys.

O'Dogan asks him if it is difficult being blond in Buenos Aires. Whether it makes him an easy target.

My assistant does not get the joke. He says Buenos Aires is full of blondes.

O'Dogan says that he knowns nothing about Buenos Aires, but he knows La Plata, the most modern city in South America, and says that that there are more blond people in Tandil than La Plata, because apart from the Spanish minority, most of the citizens are French, Italians from so far north they are almost Swiss, and particularly Danish. He nods towards a Lutheran church. It is clear he took this detour so they would pass this church. There are many Irish, too, he says, and hands my assistant his card: 'Damián O'Dogan, Public Auctioneer'.

My assistant says nothing. O'Dogan feeds him data about the only brothel in Tandil where 100% of the whores are White.

My assistant tells him that he does not patronise brothels. This is true. He wants to sound authoritative, like my wife, but it comes out wrong, like a grumble.

O'Dogan cannot help but laugh.

By this point, my assistant no longer cares about the confidential nature of his mission and comes up with a puerile plan, without considering any eventualities: to scare O'Dogan by releasing the sloth.

When they get back, my assistant runs to open the boot of the car. He tells O'Dogan that he forgot to give him a package from me.

He opens the casing and releases the sloth. O'Dogan stares at the creature, he has no idea what he is seeing and does not react to the attack.

The claw pierces the trousers and buries itself in my assistant's thigh.

O'Dogan is effusive in his offers of assistance: the hospital, the on-call nurse. He can treat the wound himself.

My assistant pushes him away. He removes the claw from the leg, lays a hand on the animal's belly and roughly plunges it back into the boot. He slams it shut and announces his departure with a shout.

It is possible that O'Dogan is asking about the package from me, because I can see his lips move as he points to the boot, seeming to have lost all interest in my assistant's wellbeing, but the sound is gone. My assistant takes his leave with a firm handshake and climbs into the car.

The infection spreads more quickly in him. By the time they reach the estate, the wound has already scabbed over and he is running a fever.

They drive through the unfinished archway at the gates. A line of trees through the scrubland marks out the overgrown driveway. No one has been here for months. The architect lied about how much progress has been made. Thankfully, this no longer matters. Let's face it, the over-elaborate project approved by the Committee had all the failings of a consensus decision.

They drive around the hill, get lost. They stop.

My assistant feels guilty that he did not anticipate the need for a machete, but this is his chance to show them who is in charge. He tells the guards to stay in the van, because of the cold, and wades through the waist-deep scrubland with a torch. His fever makes him reckless. After a few metres, he realises that he is better off without the lamp, since there is moonlight.

The house is shrouded in scaffolding. Half of the façade is still Danish, the other half has been carved with ornate arabesques and has a French mansard roof, but the wrought iron on the first-floor balconies is missing.

He creeps into the dark house. Once again, he hears his mamá's scream in the Teatro Colón. In this case, I cannot work out the link between the darkness of the house and the ebb and flow of trauma.

He flicks a light switch. In the hallway, he finds my furniture heaped into a pile, covered in plaster dust and dead leaves. In the dust, he can see the track marks of rats and pigeons. To him they look like signs traced by a finger.

He ventures to the back of the building, searching for the temporary conservatory. He finds a shed with a sagging roof.

He has everyone brought inside.

Much grumbling about the cold.

He orders the male and female Indians to be housed in separate rooms, under lock and key. He asks the guards to watch the rooms all night, at least for tonight. Tomorrow, he will draw up a rota for sentry duty and sleeping.

The maids trail after him, carrying alcohol and gauze to treat his leg. Eventually, he sits on the stairs and allows himself to be treated. They are not doing this out of a sense of duty, but simply so they can raise the subject of having separate rooms again. He waits for the first maid to bring it up, then roars at the top of his lungs for them to fuck off.

The shell has yet to be brought in. The car is about twenty metres from the house, on the edge of the forest. My assistant puts on his jacket and goes outside.

He believes the cold air on his face will alleviate his fever, but he is lurching unsteadily and he is wary of the tall grass. When he opens the car, he can smell the scent of the bodies that have travelled in it, together with my own smells.

He fumbles for the keys in the glove compartment, grabs them and, glancing up at the rear-view mirror sees the Indians perched on the unprotected balconies of the darkened house.

He tries to think what I would do. In his mind, I am older than I am, stiff as a chess piece, and dressed to the nines. He discusses his various courses of action with this puppet.

Run to the house. Implore the Indians to come inside and lock themselves in. Make them understand that this is a plea, not a threat. Summon the guards. Fire the guards first thing tomorrow. Put the blame on the maids.

To every suggestion, the puppet replies 'no' in a supercilious tone.

The Indians seem placid. There is nothing to suggest that they plan to jump. There is no need to frighten them. First, get the shell into the house, then he can decide what to do.

The puppet applauds this decision.

He opens the boot. Sees that he has not closed the shell properly. The sloth leaps at him.

He falls on his back in the mud, hugging the animal. He can feel its claws searching for a soft spot. Using his hands and feet, he thrusts it away.

The animal soars upward in a straight line, spreads its limbs, gazes at him from above, then falls back down.

He wants to let himself be hurt a little. To be cared for by the maids and the guards. To issue orders from his bed. To be pampered and pretend to be ill while he gives orders from bed.

The sloth rips off one of his nipples.

He turns and hurls himself at the animal. If he wants to, he could strangle it or break its ribs.

The puppet who is me asks him not to. He listens.

He stands up and looks down at the sloth in the mud. Luckily the nipple has caught in the fabric of his shirt. He pulls it off and holds it in his hand.

The sloth shrivels like a snail in salt. It shrieks and shudders. Shrieks and shudders.

He finds himself surrounded by the Indians. All of them, even the youngest. Their appearance is so sudden that he does not have time to scream.

They throw him down in the mud and drag him into the forest.

They take off his trousers. They want to see the wounds.

He thinks they are interested in raping him. The fear of being raped anticipates the pain of penetration in his body. This detail of the memory adds to the pleasure of the event with another orgasm.

They look at his lacerated body. The youngest Indian stands over him and whispers something that I cannot precisely translate. I recognise the words but cannot work out how to put the idea together: webbing between the fingers, doing nothing for a day, a straight metal object being inserted into wood (although the Indians are unfamiliar with metal), the action of rubbing one's eyes, and the act of coughing. To him, it sounds like a curse.

They leave him lying there and spread out, searching for the sloth, mimicking its cry.

The urgent need to get back to the house and have his wounds treated is drowned out by the thought of going back without his trousers and without the Indians. The shame becomes more intolerable than the thought of dying from an infection.

My puppet self nods, and vanishes.

My assistant gets to his feet, avoids the house and runs for half an hour through the open fields towards the hills. He never tires. Never becomes breathless.

He comes to the quarry. It is here that the event overtakes him.

This is the extent of what he recalled for my benefit.

With the poor bastard lying motionless in the quarry, the present became much less interesting than the memory he had transmitted, and much sadder because he thought he was dying.

We spent a little time doing nothing.

I noticed that the pain of the tongue bitten by the cold was not always of the same intensity and that at times the pain was his alone.

Suddenly the cold disappeared.

After that, his emotions became distinct from mine.

With the Indian, the event ended abruptly and it was a complete and utter separation. What we had been together was isolated. With my assistant it was different. The transmission of information faded in blocks, but not completely. In these gaps, the narration of things bored into my skull with ever more vivid descriptions of the night and possible animals.

After a while, the recitation disappeared in turn. We were almost free of each other.

There was no way of knowing what he was thinking or feeling, nothing. Our only link was visual information and this depended on him keeping his eyes open. When he closed his eyes, I was entirely on my side, but when he opened them again, the image reappeared.

I do not understand what follows, but it is the most important thing. I remember what follows as the most important thing.

My assistant got up. He slowly climbed down between the rocks, less awkwardly than I expected. He saw the path he had left when running through the scrubland. He retraced his steps.

He walked past the house, which was in darkness, and down the drive towards the gates. He came to the road.

From the estate to the city is about three kilometres. We walked on, looking at the landscape. He was looking at the landscape.

Between the hills, he spotted the church tower.

He came to the city square. The city was Tandil, and it was a real city, not the product of some altered consciousness, not a dream or some alien memory. But it was not the city as you and I know it. Almost, yet not.

Everything was closed, except for the little café that you and I visited together many times.

Inside, the place was a mess. Three customers were sitting at tables at the back of the café. The wood panelling was missing and the furniture was different. It was as though all decoration had been ripped away.

He sat down next to the window.

He was served by a fat man wearing a T-shirt. He looked like a Russian fresh off the boat. My assistant ordered something by tracing a circle in the air with his finger.

The Russian opened a menu and showed him a collection of circles being traced in the air, each with a price.

My assistant chose one that cost four pesos.

The Russian leaned over and unspooled a rubber cannula that extended from somewhere beneath the table and ended in a threaded metal tip. With a spray gun he took from his pocket, he moistened the tip then blew on it so it would dry.

My assistant rolled up his sleeve, took the cannula and screwed the tip into an orifice edged with something like porcelain just above his wrist. I could see that the other customers were also hooked up to cannulas, and that the Russian had a similar porcelain-edged orifice on the back of his hand.

The cannula swelled and its contents seeped into the body of my assistant, who shuddered. He began leafing through a pile of documents bearing my letterhead.

APPENDICES

APPENDICES

NATIONAL TELEPATHY COMMISSION
Buenos Aires, 1948

Mnemonic curriculum for early learning.
MN203-42. Suggested additional curricula:
MN194 and MN196-42.

The intrusionist knows and understands that her task is not to disorient by creating metaphors to describe the experience, since the required metaphors have already been judiciously chosen by Thibaud when he devised the narrative protocol; as is known, at the most basic level, the word 'event' was replaced by 'leap', evoking the leap from one person to another during the telepathic act, but was later abandoned when it was discovered that two successive wounds by the sloth do not create the 'leap' between two individuals, but between this world and a world very similar to ours in which reside our similes, versions of me and of all of you, who unknowingly receive us in their gaze.

When the event occurs between different individuals, we call it an intrusion; *between two versions of the same individual, para-intrusion.*

Other metaphors that have been discarded: the adjacent city, that of the cannulas and perfusions, since it is not separated from ours by a membrane, nor is it the obverse or reverse of any role.

For her personal well-being, the intrusionist knows and understands that the adjacent city, in this case Baires, is a determinable space of proven existence with which we maintain a unilateral escopic link by means of para-intrusion. Baires is not an illusion, nor is it the product of an altered consciousness, as Dam stated in his pioneering intrusion, nor is it triggered by drugs or the conditions of the Thibaud protocol. It is not a world mentioned in some holy book, it is not a dream.

It is easy, indeed almost biologically given to perceive Baires as unreal because, from what we know, it comprises some seventy-two percent of the same buildings and public thoroughfares, and sixty-four percent of the same citizens, of whom only one third are pure mirror-images or perfect replications, while the remainder are partial replications of types A: doppelgangers, or B: quasi-doubles or dubious cases. Confusion results from the continuous antagonism of similitude.

PRESIDENT OF THE NATION
Buenos Aires, 1951

From the President of the Nation to the Sub-Office for Urban Development.

I do not believe that to be born or raised in a single place necessarily imposes the sentence of a single view of the world, that the lands and frontiers of the State are a prison for identity, nor that the terms *Porteño, Peruvian* or *Canadian* contain a millstone whose weight bends our hand. I do not believe in the effectiveness of one, unchanging hat for all heads that seek shelter from the sun. To belong to a particular place and culture is not to be yoked to a tragic fate, but rather the capriciousness of an affair that may or may not grow into love. It is because of this very capriciousness that symbols of attachment are common in towns and cities.

In Buenos Aires, the architect Alberto Prebisch chose the most neutral form of landmark, a monolith styled as an obelisk, creating the Obelisco de Buenos Aires, a monument devoid of meaning which Porteños could symbolize according to their whim and which would serve to unify shifting identities.

Almost twenty years after the Obelisk, we urgently need to create a contemporary landmark, one that, to the urban middle classes, those least likely to vote for us and least susceptible to the plight of the oppressed classes, is a statement of egalitarian self-government.

Not a monument, but a thriving building in a constant state of flux. With living spaces, offices, public meeting rooms, a printing press, a publishing house, a public library, radio and television studios equipped with the most state-of-the-art technology available, and a nuclear bunker to protect the lives of the country's upper echelons.

Through its function, design and materials, the building should convey a message that connects every citizen to the values of the doctrine of the Peronist Movement and shapes for the better its routes, its conduct and its emblems.

The building should also enter into a dialectical discussion with the predicative plot created by other buildings in the consciousness of the citizenry.

I have had four potential sites for the New Building evaluated, according to their potential predicates and their proximity to or distance from hostile, allied or neutral buildings:

One on Avenida de Mayo, opposite the National Congress, which by chance is an empty lot.

A lot next to the CGT (Confederación General del Trabajo) Tower and the Eva Perón Foundation, in Bajo Flores.

A lot on the Avenida 9 de Julio.

A harbour in Catalinas Norte, symbolically linked to Editorial Alea.

I do not think it appropriate to purchase the lot on Avenida de Mayo, since the Movement has already set its stamp here in converting what was an upper-class avenue into a ceremonial promenade dedicated to workers, and because the New Building would set up an aerial conflict with the dome and the lighthouse on top of the Palacio Barolo (1923), a building that is a beacon to the most frivolous values of the National Centenary, whose symbolic value has waned (the lighthouse has not been in use for more than twenty years), which represents no threat or obstacle to spreading the Doctrine, and is fondly seen by the average citizen as an ornate bauble.

I do not think it advisable to purchase the lot in Bajo, as the Movement has already successfully renamed the Railway Building (1910) on Paseo Colón, the city's first high-rise building and emblem of English capital, as Ferrocarriles Argentinos following this administration's nationalisation of the railways; and, in addition, because the New Building would clash with the Edificio Libertador (1943) and take away from the prestige of the Eva Perón Foundation, just as the Foundation did with regard to the recently completed CGT building next door, which I strongly feel is the weakest point in the Movement's predicative plot, not merely because it is located far from those thoroughfares used by the average citizen, but also because it has the look of a stunted, provincial skyscraper that cloaks the noble idea of Organised Labour with a veneer of cosmopolitan affectation.

I do not think it appropriate to purchase the lot on the Avenida 9 de Julio, which common sense would blindly dictate as the ideal site for the New Building, because it would be in direct competition with an existing landmark, the Ministry of Public Works (1936), which the Movement has successfully transformed in the public imagination by making it the backdrop to numerous government ceremonies.

I recommend purchasing the harbour lot in Catalinas Norte, making the New Building the primary focal point from the river in an area already dominated by four other buildings that break the skyline: SAFICO and COMEGA, which are visible signs of the international markets, Mihanovich, an excrescence built with shipping money, and Kavanagh, built on agricultural fortunes.

SAFICO (Sociedad Anónima, Financiera y Comercial, 1934) is a sleek, modern building with a telescopic top and the frontal elevation of a Mayan temple. In the 1930s, it was a picture postcard image of the city. To the urban middle classes, it naturally represents progress, and is associated with other visual images such as the demolishing of Calle Corrientes and the construction of the abovementioned Obelisk.

COMEGA (Compañía Mercantil y Ganadera S.A., 1933) is a German building clad in travertine marble and stainless steel. It, too, features on picture postcards, most famously one involving the Graf Zeppelin flyover. The urban middle classes associate it with technical prowess, the result of an advertising campaign run twenty years ago for the building and its high-speed lifts.

Mihanovich (1918) is a palatial tower built by businessman Nicolás Mihanovich so that he could watch his shipping fleet come and go at the port for the Mihanovich Navigation Company, and crush any potential mutiny from on high. Its statement is the least powerful of the agglomeration, since it is located on a side street, with no views, but its silhouette still dominates the city's skyline from the river and its nostalgic effect on citizens who pine for an age before the doctrine should not be underestimated.

Kavanagh (1936) is not a random acronym but the surname of a cattle-ranching family carved into the only skyscraper with the status of an international landmark, the whole world's image of Argentine architecture. It appeals to the basest urges of social mobility and magical thinking: 'If I win the lottery, I'll move to the Kavanagh.' In national newspapers and tourist brochures, it was called 'the city's lofty prow', 'a metropolitan symbol' and 'a beacon of national modernism'. The building is name-checked in thirty-two novels published between 1936 and 1950: twenty-nine detective novels (in four of which the building is the scene of the crime), three romance novels and an 'experimental' novel with an erotic twist (*You Bristle in the Moist Secret of the Plains*). Its setting on a steeply sloping triangular lot makes it stand out, because it breaks the monotony of the grid, and because of the freshness of its three façades.

Given the pre-existing context, the logical way to ensure the New Building stands out would be a bold design unlike anything in the city, but this would entail breaking the sense of order familiar to the average citizen. For this reason, I suggest:

That the silhouette of the New Building follow the rectilinear geometry of the COMEGA and the SAFICO buildings, thereby completing a triad that conforms to the imagination of the international market. It should have a smooth, white façade in stark contrast to the whipped cream arabesques that adorn the capitals of the Mihanovich building.

That it borrow the idea of multiple façades from the Kavanagh, potentially adopting a triangular floor plan.

That it be clearly connected with the building housing Editorial Alea to the rear by means of a staggered ziggurat design when viewed from the Río de la Plata.

That it be constructed of noble materials and have the stature of a metropolitan manifestation of the State. Durable. The concrete flowering of a new political acumen.

That it be the tallest building in Argentina – not in South America nor the Americas as a whole: the penchant for sheer size is the banality of empire. That its height should make it a visual reference point for the national and international press. One hundred and fifty metres, topped by a telecommunications antenna breaking the skyline of Buenos Aires, as a contemporary South American gesture.

That the European city at its feet should seem like a vestige of an inequitable era.

HIS EXCELLENCY, THE PROVISIONAL PRESIDENT OF THE NATION
Buenos Aires, March 5, 1956

Prohibition of elements of ideological affirmation or Peronist propaganda.

With regard to decree 3855/55 (6) by which the Peronist Party is dissolved in its two branches by virtue of its performance and its liberticidal vocation, and

Considering:

That in its political existence the Peronist Party, acting as an instrument of the deposed regime, engaged in intensive propaganda aimed at deceiving citizens for which purpose it created images, symbols, signs and significant expressions, doctrines, articles and artistic works;

That the aforesaid objects, which were intended to disseminate a doctrine and a political position that offends the democratic sentiment of the Argentine people, constitute an affront to the latter which it is essential to eradicate, because they are a reminder of a period of suffering and contempt for the populace of the country and their use is inimical to the internal peace of the Nation and a hindrance to the strengthening of harmony among the Argentine people;

That they also affected the prestige of this country in the international arena since the doctrines and symbolic names adopted by the deposed regime sadly became synonymous with similar doctrines and names used by the great dictatorships of this century that the deposed regime continued to justify;

That these reasons make the radical suppression of these or similar instruments indispensable, and these same reasons also require the prohibition of their use in the field of trademarks and trade names, where they were also registered for advertising purposes and where their continued existence is not justified, given the vast scope of the imagination when it comes to choosing commercial logos;

Therefore, His Excellency, the Provisional President of the Argentine Nation, exercising his Legislative Power, hereby decrees with the full force of law:

Art. 1.

The following shall be prohibited throughout the territory of the Nation:

> *a) The public affirmation of Peronism, or Peronist propaganda, by any person, whether by individuals or groups of individuals, associations, unions, political parties, corporations, legal entities of public or private images, symbols, signs, meaningful expressions, doctrines, objects or artistic works that were, or could be claimed to*

have been owned or used by individuals or bodies representative of Peronism.

The following shall be considered to be in particular violation of this provision: Photography, portraiture or sculpture of Peronist officials or their relatives, the Peronist coat of arms and flag, the deposed President's own name, that of his relatives, the expressions 'Peronism', 'Peronist', 'Justicialism', 'Justicialist', 'third position', the abbreviation PP, the dates celebrated by the deposed regime, the musical compositions 'Marcha de los muchachos peronistas' and 'Evita Capitana' or fragments thereof, and the speeches of the deposed president or his wife, or fragments thereof.

b) *The use, by any person and for the purposes laid out in the foregoing paragraph, of images, symbols, signs, significant expressions, doctrine, articles and artistic works that claim status or might be considered as such, created or yet to be created, that could in any way refer to the representative individuals, organisms or ideology of Peronism.*

c) *The reproduction by any person by any process whatsoever for the purposes laid out in subparagraph (a) of images, symbols and other objects referred to in the two foregoing subparagraphs.*

Art. 2.

The provisions of the present Decree shall be declared to be public policy and consequently cannot be challenged by invoking the existence of rights acquired. All trademarks in industry, commerce and agriculture together with trade names or appurtenances consisting of the images, symbols and other objects referred to in subparagraphs (a) and (b) of Article 1 shall immediately lapse.

The respective ministries shall take all necessary measures to rescind such registrations.

Art. 3.

Whomsoever violates this decree shall be punishable by:

   a) *a term of imprisonment of between thirty days and six years, together with a fine of between M$N 500 and M$N 1,000,000;*
   b) *furthermore, such person shall be disqualified for twice the length of such sentence from working as a public official or political or trade union leader;*
   c) *furthermore, he shall be required to cease all trading activities for a period of two weeks, or in the case of a repeat offence by a commercial entity, to close definitively. Where the offence is attributable to a juridical person, the sentence may be accompanied by the dissolution of the company or entity.*

Art. 4.

The sanctions of the present Decree shall be countersigned by His Excellency the Provisional Vice-President of the Nation and by all the Secretaries of State by common accord.

Art. 5.

Copies to the Directorate General of the National Registry and archives.

Aramburu. Rojas. Busso. Podestá Costa. Landaburu. Migone. Dell'Oro Maini. Martínez. Ygartúa. Mendiondo. Bonnet. Blanco. Mercier. Alsogaray. Llamazares. Alizón García. Ossorio Arana. Hartung. Krause.

THE INTRUSIONISTS
Buenos Aires, 1957

No. D390-57. November 19. Intrusionist: Bárbara Botte. Intrusionee: Lidia Oliden. Supervisors: Brigadier Pafundo, Doctor Steimberg. Stenographer: Juan José Cabelludo.

Section A

I describe the session according to the Thibaud protocol.

Oliden burst into the intrusion chamber in a state of feverish exaltation. She was placed in a standing position and restrained using an abdominal strap, a jaw restraint and a leg-spreader. The fitting of the leg-spreader shut her up.

I stood facing her, adopting the same stance and winked to reassure her that everything was alright. I explained the duration and purpose of the process:

To collect any and all data that might implicate or exonerate her as an agent working for foreign intelligence, an adherent to anti-Argentine activities, or an independent traitor.

The duration of the Intrusion: less than two hours.

The basic concepts of intrusionism.

Thibaud's protocols and code of conduct for work done by the Commission.

Acceptance of conditions and characteristics of this work as privileged by state secrecy.

Compulsory provisional induction into the body of intrusionists of the National Telepathy Commission.

To reassure her that everything was alright, I strapped on my own jaw restraint and we were equal.

Blood was drawn and injected into sloth number eight.

The intrusion began at 19:04 hours.

During the preliminary phase, Oliden received a mnesic set from me comprising the following memories from my belonging:

An eventful trip to Sunchales, a direct encounter with cows on the road, stroking the cows.

Spending an afternoon weaving a decorative tapestry.

Cooking milanesa de peceto.

Oliden calmed down. Simultaneously, I received her inarticulate mnesic set, from which the data in section b of this report is drawn.

In the first phase of intrusion, the intrusionee presented symptoms of visual distortion, dizziness and nausea. In previous reports, several intrusionists have raised the problem of conducting intrusions when both parties are in the same room. It is easier to receive information from two discrete locations than from the same location observed by two people in close proximity. We suggest that, at the very least, the two halves of the room be painted in clearly differentiated colours.

The second phase was disrupted by the physical pain of the abdominal strap and the excessive spread of the legs. Several intrusionists have already suggested to Dr Steimberg that abdominal restraints are unnecessary because, during the initial session, the subject does not acquire the vaginal mobility required for geniphrasis. We hope this will be taken into account for future sessions.

At the end of the intrusion, the intrusionee showed signs of exhaustion caused by intense pleasure and required medical attention. Her condition was stabilised.

Section B

Lidia Oliden, 27 years old, Argentine, born in Buenos Aires. Third level education at the National Music Conservatory. A course in typing and speed reading at the Ilvem Institute. Private piano tutor with no clients over the past year. Former shop assistant at Harrods, dismissed for suspected theft.

In view of this report, Brigadier Pafundo and Dr Steimberg provisionally absolve the intrusionee of responsibility for publicly leaking the location of this office via a fake advertisement in *La Nación*. Weekly follow-up sessions are recommended until her innocence has been substantiated.

Given this first intrusive experience, it is impossible to release the patient without jeopardising the security of this office. She must be immediately integrated into the staff of intrusionists.

Section C

Background: Oliden introduced herself as an aspiring employee of the Commission following a fake advertisement which divulged the location of this agency, thereby exposing it to impromptu visits that might have been a pretext for an attack or an attempt to infiltrate the Commission.

Her arrest was ordered because her name did not appear on the official list of applicants.

The following information was obtained via intrusion by mnesic retrogradation, according to Thibaud's order of priority.

She spent the last six months of the current year as a shop assistant on the fifth floor of Harrods, working Monday to Sunday, and national holidays from 2 p.m. to 10 p.m. She sold ladies' accessories.

Five minutes before closing, López, the floor manager, summoned the salesgirls and showed them an umbrella from the 'Mademoiselle' collection of reissued thirties' designs. He explained how to go about selling it as a luxury object. The ribs of the umbrella were carved from solid mahogany and curved like the branches of a tree in a Japanese print. It was available in four modish colours. The fabric was the most waterproof on the market and could withstand more than half an hour of continuous rain without leaking inside like an ordinary umbrella. They should suggest that customers have their initials engraved on the handle of the umbrella. The engraving service offered by Harrods could process the order within two to three days.

Oliden could see that López was staring at her as he spoke. She interrupted to ask him why. López explained that he was staring at her because when speaking in public, it is best to look at someone whose face is the face of everyone, and that it was difficult not to stare at her, for obvious reasons. Some of the other staff laughed at this remark.

The following day a 'Mademoiselle' umbrella was stolen from Oliden's department. Señor López sent for a stool so he would be the same height as she was, and declared that given her height, she could see the whole department, so it was impossible that she had not witnessed the theft. He accused her of being an accomplice.

Oliden slapped him and knocked him off the stool.

She said goodbye to her colleagues, and took her belongings from her locker: a tortoiseshell comb and a fake pearl necklace she had bought at Harrods using her staff discount.

She went home. She lives with her father in a three-room flat in the attic of the Edificio Femenil on Avenida Rivadavia. Her father is a vet working with dogs. She did not tell him that she had been fired.

Over dinner, her father gave a detailed account of how Pomeranian dogs were crossbred so that their size was reduced from medium to miniature in less than a century.

From that dinner I obtained the information that:

Neither of them believes in God. She, out of loyalty to an anarchist grandfather she never knew. He, according to her, out of spiritual dullness. Neither has any interest in any anti-patriotic movements. They know nothing about communism or anarchism, not even through the aforementioned grandfather, and they have no particular opinion about Peronism.

For the next three days Oliden pretended to go to Harrods and instead checked the newspapers for work at a café two blocks from her house.

On that particular morning she saw the advertisement in *La Nación*.

Edificio Alas (formerly ATLAS), Secretariat of Aeronautics.
Required: exceptional young woman, 25-35 years old, single, with excellent shorthand and typing skills. Apply in person between 8 a.m. and 12 noon on Wednesday, April 3rd. Office 9, Floor 37, 719 Avenida Alem.

Tram delays meant that she arrived at the last minute. As she was crossing Avenida Alem, she spotted a girl with a very prominent chin and an albino girl wearing the same shoes as she was. To Oliden they, too, seemed 'exceptional' (Oliden is very tall) and all three fit the requirements of the advertisement. She followed them into the building and all three took the lift.

The albino was Elsa Letelier, niece of Vice-Commodore Letelier, who had just joined the Commission. The girl with the protruding chin was Ángeles Aguirre, who had joined the Commission a month earlier on the recommendation of Dr Steimberg.

In the lift, Oliden asked if they knew what the job entailed. They found it curious that she did not seem to know anything. Oliden explained that she had only just seen the advertisement in the paper. Letelier gave a nervous giggle that lasted about six or seven seconds – too long for an exchange between strangers. As a result, via a peri-descriptive subroutine, Oliden concluded that the albino was from the upper-middle-class. She had encountered many customers just like her. Their mothers taught them to laugh like that. They bought white underwear.

The image of white underwear in a dresser drawer evoked an image of her own dresser and she remembered that she had forgotten her ID card and her shorthand and typing certificate from the Ilvem Institute.

On the ninth floor, Brigadier Pafundo stepped into the lift in mufti, dressed in a tailored tweed suit. Oliden looked away from him and flinched as though she had been slapped. This is a common reaction to beauty.

As the doors closed, the forceful aroma of the Brigadier's Brylcreem filled the lift and triggered in Oliden a libidinal withdrawal effect.

Pafundo jabbed a finger towards her and asked who she was. Before Oliden could reply, he asked Ángeles Aguirre, who said she did not know her.

Pafundo asked to see her documents and she explained that she had forgotten them.

They reached the thirty-seventh floor.

The Brigadier and Ángeles Aguirre restrained Oliden and dragged her to the intrusion chamber. They forced her to sit facing the window and watch the city swathed in smoke from the incinerators until I was ready.

Oliden suffered a rapid drop in blood pressure and fits of crying. The board of intrusionists has frequently pointed out that the interrogations provide clearer data when the patient is calm. Her arrest could have been less brutal.

Section D

A mnesic set of welcome and introduction. It is a precise reproduction of that made by Dr Steimberg in July 1956.

As intrusionists, we have suggested to Dr Steimberg on numerous occasions that this memory be replaced by one that includes the new regulations put in place over the past year.

> *Welcome. If you are receiving this information, it is because you have agreed to be part of this experimental protocol and because you have answered the following questions in writing: Do you suffer from any form of cardiovascular disease? Do you use or have you been prescribed any psychiatric medications? Are you a member of any political group? Do you suffer from visual or auditory hallucinations? Do you believe in God? Would you describe*

yourself as a cowardly person? Do you know how to use a firearm? Do you drive a car? The answers you provide will determine the role you will play in the team of intrusionists and which part of the office you will be assigned.

The failure rate of the protocol is low and risks are minimal. Principally behavioural disorders. As a general rule, a fortnightly check-up with the Commission's neurologist is sufficient to maintain the stability of the intrusionist. Visits to the neurologist are compulsory. His consulting room is located on the thirty-second floor.

The apprentice intrusionist conducts intrusions of vital importance to public security and national intelligence. Advanced intrusionists conduct more complex para-intrusive missions. The intrusionist corps is at the service of the National Telepathy Commission, a division of the Secretariat of Aeronautics. All work falls under the status of state secret.

Advanced intrusionists are permitted to reside outside the building. Apprentices are housed on the thirty-fifth floor, and are allowed to visit friends or relatives twice a month, with the proviso that they do not go beyond the borders of the Federal Capital of Buenos Aires. A condition of such visits is that the intrusionist assume a false identity agreed between her and the Commission.

The National Telepathy Commission was founded by Dr Hilario Thibaud in 1937, under the provisional name of the 'Segundo Jorge Dam Intrusion Committee', in honour of the father of Amado Dam, the driving force behind this project and pioneering intrusionist.

When Dam died of an infection in 1939, Dr Thibaud re-founded the commission under its current name and it was integrated into the State as a secret agency. It operated out of offices in the Railway Building, a stone's throw from the Casa Rosada, until the Perón government nationalised the railways and renamed the building the Edificio de Ferrocarriles Argentinos. During the reign of this dictator, the Commission was on the verge of losing its offices and being forced to perform public tasks under the ridiculous demand of 'bringing it closer to the people'.

Our collaboration with the Armed Forces of the Argentine Republic brought the tyrant's rule to an end.

By way of reward, the current government commandeered this building, the beacon and symbol of 'Peronist progress', assigned it to the Secretariat of Aeronautics, and changed the name of the building from Edificio ATLAS, an acronym for the Peronist 'Agrupación de Trabajadores Latinoamericanos Sociedad Anónima', to ALAS – Wings – in tribute to the heroic pilots who bombed the Plaza de Mayo to ensure the freedom of this country. The T in ATLAS became a secret, a metaphor for the workings of the National Telepathy Commission in the new offices.

For the foregoing reasons, the building evokes a certain nostalgia among those who long for proscribed Peronism.

Any inquisitive person seeking admittance under the pretext of wanting to photograph the tallest building in the city is immediately suspect.

Any unscheduled intrusion is treated as an attack. Our intrusionists are trained to create mnesic sets or pre-programmed memories that block access to any sensitive information during the first phase of the intrusion.

No adequate block has been devised for the second phase. The protocol therefore requires immediate sedation. The intrusionist is authorised to carry a syringe and a sedative just as a police officer carries a service revolver.

This field of study that we strive to control on a daily basis generates its own terminology and we have an extensive ad hoc glossary to accurately describe it. The intrusionist is required to know and use these terms without error.

No D422-57. December 12. Intrusionist: Bárbara Botte. Subject: Lidia Oliden. Supervisors: Brigadier Pafundo, Doctor Steimberg. Stenographer: Juan José Cabelludo.

To create a blocking mnesic set for Oliden, I selected three of her own memories:

Practising musical scales with a child from Caballito in the morning.
Comparing the weight of a hat and a briefcase. They feel the same. This is something she has previously experienced with a pencil and a mug.
Eight minutes of praise from her father of the English sewage system in Buenos Aires.

I succeeded in implanting the musical scale during the first phase, over the course of two consecutive sessions, but the other two memories were not successfully embedded and left perilogical links exposed that connected to memories of her present life in the building.

As a result of this setback, Dr Steimberg decided to continue with the subject's training and not to promote her to conducting professional intrusions.

No D590-57. 22 December. Intrusionist: Bárbara Botte. Subjects: Lidia Oliden, Elsa Letelier, Ángeles Aguirre. Supervisors: Brigadier Pafundo, Doctor Steimberg. Stenographer: Juan José Cabelludo.

Section A

Below, I describe the session in accordance with the Thibaud protocol. Linking priority routine: level three facts and/or information.

Background: in accordance with the Thibaud protocols relating to threats and tracking, simultaneous intrusions involving three subjects were organised to confirm or rule out the possibility that the intrusionist corps were the source of the fake advertisement published in *La Nación*. The session detailed in this report included subjects Elsa Letelier (Level 1), Ángeles Aguirre (Level 3) and Lidia Oliden (In Training).

In the first phase, Letelier isolated a memory in which Aguirre dictated the wording of the fake advertisement by geniphrasis to Nilda Ordóñez, a cleaner who was tidying her room while Aguirre, her legs splayed, was pretending to shave.

Having been unmasked, Aguirre tried to escape from the chamber, hurling all manner of objects at Brigadier Pafundo and Dr Steimberg. They successfully restrained her, but during the struggle Pafundo was thrown against the pod containing sloth number twelve, which broke as he fell. The sloth emerged from the pile of glass and crept across the floor until it reached the feet of Lidia Oliden, who snatched up the animal and threatened to suffocate it if she was not permitted to leave.

The sloth twisted around and slashed Oliden's chest and stomach. As a result, Oliden, together with Letelier, were exposed to an unscheduled para-intrusion with me. Both required oxygen during the session.

Section B

The para-intrusive episode. No new data on perforations, porcelain and perfusions. New data: nylon. This confirms the hypothesis of para-intrusive reports O132/45/77-57: Baires exists precisely 34 days in the past. The present para-intrusion corresponds to the day before Oliden was fired from Harrods.

She is serving in the ladies' lingerie department. She takes a pair of nylons and stretches them in front of three customers. Given the extreme nature of the stretching and the customers' fascination, it is clear that the fabric is being presented as something new. She sells two pairs of nylon stockings, one black, one flesh-coloured.

The floor manager, Señor López (full replication to be confirmed), walks over and leads the female staff into the staffroom.

Before the meeting begins, López and a number of the sales assistants take cannulas from beneath a table, screw them into their respective porcelain orifices and shudder.

López brandishes an umbrella identical to the one described in report *No. D390-57* as a 'Mademoiselle'. In this case, the label says 'Señorita'. He opens it, closes it, explains and demonstrates how the mechanism works.

Oliden notices that López is staring at her. She interrupts and asks why. López tells her that when speaking in public it is best to look at someone whose face is the face of everyone.

Buenos Aires, 2020

Director & Editor: Carolina Orloff
Director: Samuel McDowell

www.charcopress.com

The National Telepathy was published on
80gsm Munken Premium Cream paper.

The text was designed using Bembo 11.5 and ITC Galliard.

Printed in August 2024 by TJ Books
Padstow, Cornwall, PL28 8RW using responsibly
sourced paper and environmentally-friendly adhesive.